Where had they gone?
Emma wondered.

What had become of the men and women who had lived in this city?

For a moment she felt an almost overwhelming sadness for the people who had lived in this ancient place.

With a sigh, telling herself she was being foolish, she put the last photograph in the developing fluid. Slowly, slowly, the pyramid emerged from the chemicals, the top half of it lost in the clouds. And through the clouds she saw the figure of Miguel Rivas, descending like a god of old from the clouds of heaven.

"The cloud man," she said under her breath, and she knew that was the way she would always think of him. For, though he was a modern man, there was a part of him that seemed not to belong in the modern world, a part of him that surely came from another, older, civilization....

Dear Reader,

Once again, we've rounded up a month of top-notch reading for you—just right for the hot weather! Heather Graham Pozzessere, a *New York Times* bestselling author, has penned our American Hero title, *Between Roc and a Hard Place.* This is the story of a not-quite-divorced couple who meet up again in a very...unique way. And once they do, boy! The sparks really start flying then—and you'll want to be there to catch all the action.

The rest of the month is pretty special, too. Marie Ferrarella returns with the second title in her series called "Those Sinclairs!" *Heroes Great and Small* is a fitting follow-up to last month's *Holding Out for a Hero.* And later in the year look for brother Nik's story in *Christmas Every Day.* Dallas Schulze makes a welcome return appearance in the line with *Secondhand Husband,* a tale of love growing—as I guess it always does—in strange and mysterious ways. Finish off your reading with Barbara Faith's *Cloud Man* (this hero makes an absolutely unforgettable entrance), Desire author Cathryn Clare's *Chasing Destiny* and new author Debbie Bryce's *Edge of Darkness.* As always, it's a lineup of books so good you'll want to read every one.

And in coming months, look for more great romantic reading here at Intimate Moments, with books by favorite authors like Naomi Horton, Justine Davis, Emilie Richards, Marilyn Pappano and Doreen Roberts, to name only a few. Join us!

Yours,

Leslie Wainger
Senior Editor and Editorial Coordinator

CLOUD MAN

Barbara Faith

Silhouette®

INTIMATE MOMENTS®

Published by Silhouette Books New York

America's Publisher of Contemporary Romance

SILHOUETTE BOOKS
300 East 42nd St., New York, N.Y. 10017

CLOUD MAN

Copyright © 1993 by Barbara Faith

All rights reserved. Except for use in any review, the reproduction or utilization of this work in whole or in part in any form by any electronic, mechanical or other means, now known or hereafter invented, including xerography, photocopying and recording, or in any information storage or retrieval system, is forbidden without the permission of the publisher, Silhouette Books, 300 E. 42nd St., New York, N.Y. 10017

ISBN: 0-373-07502-2

First Silhouette Books printing June 1993

All the characters in this book have no existence outside the imagination of the author and have no relation whatsoever to anyone bearing the same name or names. They are not even distantly inspired by any individual known or unknown to the author, and all incidents are pure invention.

®: Trademark used under license and registered in the United States Patent and Trademark Office and in other countries.

Printed in the U.S.A.

BARBARA FAITH

is a true romantic who believes that love is a rare and precious gift. She has an endless fascination with the attraction a man and a woman from different cultures and backgrounds have for each other. She considers herself a good example of such an attraction, because she has been happily married for over twenty years to an ex-matador she met when she lived in Mexico.

For Las Sylvias.
And once again, for Alfonso.

A Note from the Author
The mountainous state of Oaxaca, pronounced
"wa-HA-ka," is in southern Mexico. The city is also
named Oaxaca.

Chapter 1

It was as though she had stepped back three thousand years in time, back to when this ancient city of Monte Alban had been at its zenith.

She stood alone on the rise of land that overlooked the ruins. In a way she could not explain, it seemed to her that she could almost see the city as it had been, and that if she listened very closely she might hear children playing there in the square, and the vendors—the sweetmeat sellers, the feather merchants and the pottery makers—calling out to one another.

Not easily given to flights of fancy, Emma Pilgrim smiled and shook her head. Like her banker father she believed in what she could see, hear and verify, and in what could scientifically or mathematically be proven.

There had been a time when she'd wanted to be like her mother, but as she'd grown older she'd known she never would be. Penelope Pilgrim, a beautiful butterfly of a woman who looked not unlike the fairy god-mother in *Cinderella,* wrote children's books, imaginative stories of adventure in fairy-tale lands where anything was possible.

When her daughter had been born, Penelope wanted to name her Annabel Lee because, she'd said, "Mr. Poe's Annabel Lee had no other thought than to love and be loved. Now isn't that nice?" But James had insisted his daughter be named Emma after his mother, and as she always did, Penelope had given in to him.

Which was just as well, because Emma didn't look like an Annabel Lee, she looked like an Emma. At five foot seven, she was half a foot taller than her mother. Her hair wasn't blond and curly, it was autumn brown and straight as a stick. Her eyes were green, her nose was patrician, her mouth was firm.

"A no-nonsense kind of woman with a level head on her shoulders," her father would say proudly. And every time he did, Penelope sighed.

A free-lance writer and photographer, Emma wrote mostly for scientific journals. She had come to Oaxaca in southern Mexico to do a series of articles on the archaeological sites in and around the region. Monte Alban and Mitla were the major sites, of course, but there were other important ruins as well, and Emma planned to stay in the city of Oaxaca until she had visited and photographed all of them.

Now, as she moved down to the ball court, toward the Gran Plaza, she consulted her notes. Nearly one hundred and seventy tombs, she read, many with elaborate and decorated frescoes, had been uncovered over the years. Pottery depicting Zapotec gods

had been found, as well as jade urns, turquoise necklaces and wonderfully elaborate gold pendants.

Most of these valuable artifacts were in the Museum of Anthropology in Mexico City, and a few were
here in the Monte Alban Museum. But over the years
many of these ancient treasures had been stolen and
sold to collectors all over the world.

In tomb number 74 Emma studied the stone figures
of the God of Corn and the God of Renewal that had
been carved into the wall of the tomb. The God of
Corn, with its headdress made to look like corn leaves,
was magnificent in its strength. But it was the figure
of the God of Renewal that stopped Emma where she
stood.

It had a fierceness of beauty that took her breath.
The stone was rough and cool to her touch. The
slanted eyes, wise with the passage of time, looked out
at her. The god-man's cheekbones were high, the jut-
ting nose was strong, the mouth wide, the lips full.

Octavio Paz, in his *Labyrinth of Solitude,* had spoken of the Mexican mask. "The Mexican," Paz said,
"seems to me to be a person who shuts himself away
to protect himself. In his harsh solitude, which is both
barbed and courteous, everything serves him as a de-
fense.... He can bend, can bow humbly, can even
stoop, but he cannot back down."

Emma had read the passage many times, but she
had not understood it until now, for as she looked at
the figure before her, she knew that this god-man
would never back down.

Strangely moved, she took a deep breath and
stepped back to study the whole figure. His body was

strong, and masculine. His male member was large; his feet were the claws of an eagle.

There were other carvings here, but each time she looked away she found herself glancing back. Though she knew there were many other things to see, she was reluctant to leave. She touched his face again, then made herself turn and walk out into the sunlight.

Back once more on the grassy plain, she moved past the palace and the temples, the ball court and the platforms, lost in thought as she gazed at the ancient buildings, her imagination captured as the late-afternoon sun slowly descended behind the pyramid. In a little while she went off to the side of the ruins to an overhang of rocks. Below her lay the valley of Oaxaca and the city, somnolent in the setting sun.

She did not know how long she stood there looking out at the mountains and the city, but suddenly the breeze picked up, and the sky, which only a few moments before had been a hazy blue, darkened. She looked at her watch, and when she saw that it was six-thirty, she frowned.

She had come out to Monte Alban on a tour bus that morning, but as soon as she'd arrived, she'd left the others and set out to explore on her own. Now the driver's words came back to her. "We will leave at exactly five-thirty from in front of the museum," he had said. "Do not be late. There is no other transportation to the city and it's a long walk."

Wonderful, Emma thought as she left her place on the rocky ledge and started back toward the grassy plain. In the distance she heard the roll of thunder. Dark clouds formed and lowered and there was a chill in the air.

It was then she realized that she was alone. The ruins were deserted; there was no one about, no guard, not even a stray dog. Strangely enough, she liked the feeling. It gave her a better sense of this city that had been abandoned by the Zapotec Indians somewhere between A.D. 700 and 800. By the time the Mixtecs came, probably between A.D. 1100 and 1300, there had not been a trace of the earlier people. Why? Emma wondered. What had happened to them? Where had they gone?

She thought of the God of Renewal and of the man he had perhaps been modeled after. Where had he gone, that centuries-old man?

She stood lost in thought for a little while, then took the camera she had slung around her neck and began to take pictures. She had planned only to get a feel of the place today, but the light and shadows were good, and the lowering clouds so threatening they added a sense of mystery to this already mysterious place. She photographed the platforms, the stairs and the columns, then turned once again to the pyramid and began to photograph it.

Thunder cracked. A bolt of lightning snaked through the darkening sky and the clouds that covered the top half of the pyramid. Emma focused, snapped, and moved closer. It was hauntingly beautiful. It . . .

She froze, unable to believe her eyes, for suddenly a figure emerged from the clouds, climbing down the narrow steps of the pyramid.

Transfixed, Emma stared up at the man who moved slowly toward her. He was tall, appearing more elongated from her position below him. He stopped midway down. She knew that he had seen her, but still caught somewhere between the past and the present, between a dream of what once had been and the reality of the here and now, she didn't move.

He reached the bottom step and started toward her, his face still obscured in the advancing dusk. He wore the white cotton pants, white shirt and straw sandals that was the dress of the local Indians.

He drew closer, and when he was but a few feet away, he said in Spanish, "What are you doing here? This place is closed."

Emma wet her lips, too startled for a moment to speak. The man before her was tall, and slim as a reed. He had a narrow face, high cheekbones and dark, slightly slanted eyes. His hair was Indian black. He looked foreign, different from any other man, and as she stood there in that ancient place, she wondered if, by some fluke of nature or time, he was one of that race of people who had vanished from here hundreds of years ago.

He looked from her to her camera. "Well, *señorita?*" he said in English.

And Emma, who had never stammered in her life, stammered, "I—I came out on the tour bus."

"It left over an hour ago."

"I forgot the time. I . . ."

Thunder growled and a sudden gust of wind blew the dust around them, lifting her full skirt, swirling it around her bare legs.

"It's going to storm," he said.

"Yes." She tried to hold her skirt down. "I have to look for a taxi."

"There aren't any taxis, at least not up here." He frowned. "I'll have to drive you to Oaxaca."

Because she had seen his frown, Emma shook her head. "I can walk," she said.

"Nonsense. It's almost six miles."

It began to spatter rain. The man took Emma's arm, and before she could say anything else, he started across the plaza toward the entrance of the ruins. By the time they reached the rocky crest that led to the museum and the parking lot below, the spatter became fat, heavy drops. He gripped Emma's hand, and together they raced toward the parking place and the lone car that was parked there. The rain came harder. He unlocked the door and helped her in. By the time he had run around to the driver's side, the rain had become a deluge.

He muttered a word in Spanish Emma didn't understand, then in English said, "I'm afraid we'll have to sit it out, *señorita*. It's raining too hard to try to get down the mountain." He looked at the long straight hair hanging down over her shoulders. "I'm sorry I don't have a towel."

"No, it's all right, I barely got wet." Emma brushed her hair back with her hands. Lightning flashed and he saw her face, her wide green eyes, her full lips parted as a crash of thunder shook the car.

"Don't be alarmed. This can't last long." And because he knew she was uncomfortable with him, he said, "Permit me to introduce myself. My name is Miguel Rivas."

"Emma Pilgrim." She offered a tentative smile. "Thank you for rescuing me. I don't know what I

would have done in a storm like this. I'm afraid I'd
have had to swim to the city."

"It would have been a long swim." He allowed
himself an answering smile and eased back against the
door. "Where are you from, Señorita Pilgrim."

"Denver."

"You have come to Oaxaca for a vacation?"

Emma shook her head. "I'm a writer and a photographer, and I'm here on an assignment." Rain
slashed hard against the windows of the car. "Are you
from Oaxaca, Mr. Rivas?"

"From the state, yes. I have a house in the city and
a *choza* in the hills where I try to spend most weekends."

"A *choza?*" Emma asked, puzzled.

"It's a rustic cabin with a palm-thatched roof, Miss
Pilgrim. Near a remote Indian village where there is no
running water or electricity."

"But why...?" He wore Indian clothes, but he had
obviously gotten his education elsewhere. And she
didn't think Indians drove late-model, air-conditioned
cars. Why then did he choose to live and dress like an
Indian?

"Tell me about the articles you will write," he said.
"Are they for women's magazines?"

"Women's magazines?" Emma raised an eyebrow.
"I write for scientific journals. I came here to do a series of articles on Monte Alban and Mitla, as well as
the other archaeological sites in the area."

"Scientific journals?"

A gust of wind slammed against the car. Emma
drew her breath in sharply, and said, "I'm interested
in what happened to the Zapotec Indians who lived

here so long ago. I believe there's a scientific explanation for everything and I—"

"A scientific reason?" A smile that was not altogether friendly curved the corners of Miguel Rivas's mouth. "There are many things in this world that cannot be explained by science, *señorita* "

"I don't believe that." She lifted her chin. "There has to be a logical reason—"

Another great rush of thunder jolted the car. Emma flinched, and without thinking, grabbed at Miguel's arm.

"It's all right," he said. "The storm is almost over."

"It doesn't sound like it's over." She took her hand away. "Sorry. I don't usually act this way."

He believed her. There was something in the set of her jaw that told him she was capable under most circumstances of taking care of herself. He was not sure, though, that he believed her reason for being in Oaxaca. The fact that she had stayed behind at the ruins after everyone else had left, especially when a storm was threatening, aroused his suspicions. As did the camera.

Strange things had been happening since the discovery of the new tomb two months ago. In addition to the men who regularly patrolled the site, an extra guard had been hired. Though the day guards left at six, one was supposed to stay until his replacement arrived. But there hadn't been any sign of a guard when he'd come down from the pyramid, only this American woman with her camera. He didn't like it.

The rain slackened. He decided he'd better have a look around before he left, but just as he said,

"There's something I want to check on," an ancient pickup drove into the parking lot.

"I'll only be a minute," he told Emma, and opening his door, he hurried over to the guard.

"*Buenas tardes,* Salvador," he said.

"*Buenas tardes,* Señor Rivas. *¿Que tal?* How is everything? This was some kind of a storm, no?"

"Yes, it was." Miguel looked toward the ruins. "Where is the other guard? I didn't see him before I left."

"Manuel?" Salvador pushed his straw hat back and scratched his head. "He leaves at six, *señor.*"

"And you're supposed to arrive at six?"

"*Sí,* but I was delayed by the storm. I'm sorry, Señor Rivas. It is my fault."

"No, it isn't. Manuel should stay until you arrive, no matter how late you are. You tell him that when he relieves you in the morning. If he has a problem with it, we'll get somebody else. The same goes for you, Salvador. You're not to leave until he relieves you in the morning. Is that clear?"

"*Pero—*"

"Is that clear?" Miguel repeated.

"*Sí.*" The man shuffled his feet and muttered, "Yes, all right, I understand."

"Very well." Miguel turned away and over his shoulder said, "We will talk again later."

Emma had watched the two men. She had understood most of the conversation, enough to realize that Rivas had been angry and that very likely he worked here at the ruins.

He came back to the car, brushed his wet hair off his forehead impatiently and said, "We can go now."

The narrow road down from the ruins was slick with rain and mud. He drove carefully, mumbling to himself that he should have taken the Jeep, but did not speak to Emma until they were on the main road that led to town.

"It's late." He shot her a look. "Are you hungry?"

"Yes," she said without thinking. She'd had a fruit salad before she'd left the hotel, but that had been at noon. It was almost seven-thirty now.

Rivas swerved when a boy on a bicycle darted out around him. He cursed, then said, "If you're not in a hurry, I know a place you might like."

"That's very nice of you, Mr. Rivas, but—"

"Miguel," he said. And before Emma could object, he swung the car into a restaurant driveway. An attendant hurried over and opened the door.

The restaurant looked elegant, too elegant for the sundress and sandals she was wearing.

"I look like a drowned rat and my hair is all wet and straggly," she objected.

"So is mine," he said.

Emma looked at him. His thick black hair was as smooth and slick as a seal's. It was the kind of hair that was never out of place. There wasn't anything straggly about him. In spite of the rain he'd been in, he looked almost bandbox perfect.

The attendant ran around to her side of the car and opened the door. She had no choice but to say, "Thank you," and let Miguel Rivas lead her into the restaurant.

"Don Miguel!" A white-haired man hurried over to clasp Miguel Rivas's hand. "How good it is to see you.

We've missed you." He smiled at Emma. "*Buenas noches, señorita.* Welcome to La Casa Ruiz." He smiled. "I am Paco Ruiz, at your service."

He led them to a secluded corner table, lighted the center candle with a flourish and said, "*¿Dos margaritas?*"

Miguel looked at her. "Yes?" he asked. When Emma hesitated, he said, "For the rain. It will help you to not catch a cold." And when she nodded, he said, "Two margaritas, Paco. *Gracias.*"

The margaritas were good, the conversation stilted. Emma excused herself long enough to repair her face and brush her shoulder-length hair, fastening it back with a clasp from her purse. She felt strange being here with a man she didn't know, but she wasn't quite sure what to do about it. She would, of course, pay for her own dinner, and as soon as they had finished, would take a cab to her hotel.

He rose to hold her chair when she returned to the table. "I took the liberty of ordering," he said. "The *carne asada* is very good here. Is that all right?"

"Yes, that will be fine." And because she couldn't think of anything else to say, she asked, "Do you work at Monte Alban, Señor Rivas?"

"Sometimes." He took a sip of his drink. "I'm an archaeologist, Miss Pilgrim. My work takes me to many of the sites in the area, as well as to other parts of Mexico. I've been concentrating my efforts at Monte Alban these past few weeks because a new tomb was discovered two months ago. It's an exciting find. We're just now beginning to bring out some of the artifacts." He hesitated, studying her, and in a casual voice said, "That's why I was surprised when I saw you earlier. There should have been a guard on duty to tell you that it was long past closing time."

"A new tomb?" she said, ignoring his comment about the guard. "That's pretty exciting, isn't it?"

Miguel nodded. "And possibly dangerous."

"Dangerous?"

"There have already been attempts to rob the new tomb." Miguel finished his drink and put the empty glass next to his plate. "There are collectors in the United States and Europe, as well as in Mexico, who would be willing to pay great sums of money for the artifacts."

Emma toyed with her spoon. "People collect all sorts of things," she said after a moment or two. "I can't really see that artifacts are very much different than art, if a collector truly appreciates beautiful things, I mean." She looked at him. "My father is a collector," she said. "He has some wonderful pieces, from Peru, Turkey, Greece and Egypt. He—"

Miguel's dark eyes were suddenly as cold as ice. No, Emma thought, as cold and hard as the stone eyes of the God of Renewal she had seen earlier.

"Artifacts are the history of a country," he said. "The legacy of a people who have gone before. To sell or barter pieces of history would be like selling or bartering pieces of ourselves."

"I understand your feelings." Emma pressed the white linen napkin to her lips. "But—"

"There is no but," Miguel snapped. "To buy and sell an artifact is a criminal offense."

"If you're saying my father is a criminal . . ." Her green eyes flashed him a warning.

"I don't know your father." Miguel leaned across the table, his gaze never leaving hers. "Perhaps he didn't know that what he was doing was wrong, but it was wrong, Miss Pilgrim. Believe me, it was wrong."

They finished the rest of the meal in silence. When their waiter brought the check, Emma tried to pay her part of it. Miguel wouldn't let her. He looked annoyed that she even tried.

Actually, he thought as he reached for his wallet, there were several things about this *gringa* that annoyed him. Her cavalier attitude about artifacts for one, her certainty that all the mysteries of Monte Alban could be scientifically explained for another.

He would keep an eye on her, he decided. If she and her father were up to something, he'd stop them before they started. If she even looked like she was going to steal an artifact, he'd personally see to it that she spent the next ten years sweating it out in a Mexican prison.

Just then she raised her glass to take a last sip of her water, and he looked at her mouth. He saw the softness, the vulnerability there. And something quite unexpected happened—a slight catch of his breath, a clutching feeling somewhere deep inside him.

Nonsense, he told himself, even as he decided that keeping an eye on Miss Emma Pilgrim might not be such an unpleasant job after all.

Chapter 2

The Posada Cortez was one block off the *zocalo,* the town square. Emma's room on the second floor was clean and light, but by noon unbearably hot. She had heard that summer in southern Mexico was warm, but she had not expected this kind of devastating heat. Three days of it were enough, she decided the night of her encounter with Miguel Rivas. Tomorrow the studio and apartment she had rented through a visual artists' organization she belonged to would be ready, and she would move in.

She had placed an ad in the organization's newsletter last winter. Two months ago she had received a letter from a Señor Ernesto Sauto in Oaxaca, saying that he would rent her his fully equipped studio and apartment for the months of June and July.

She had gone to the apartment as soon as she arrived in Oaxaca. It was on a quiet street only a few blocks from the *zocalo,* and although it did not have the air-conditioning she had hoped for, there were ceiling fans. Señor Sauto had shown her around. The photo studio was in better shape than the apartment, and while some of the equipment was not as up-to-date as what she was used to, it was certainly adequate.

The apartment itself was shabby and rundown. The living room was small, the white paint on the wicker furniture chipped. There was a double bed and a dresser in the small bedroom and, fortunately, enough utensils in the kitchen to cook a simple meal. For a reason Emma could not understand, the refrigerator wasn't in the kitchen but in the studio.

It was very warm when Emma awoke in her room at the hotel the next morning. She had a cup of tea and decided that she would go to the market and buy a straw hat before she checked out. If she was going to be out in the sun today, she would need a hat for protection.

The indoor market was a colorful maze of crowded aisles and stands. Fruits and vegetables were arranged in a rainbow of colors. Indian dresses hung from hangers over the stalls; black pottery, green pottery, paper flowers, serapes and blankets were all displayed. Women worked at back-strap looms, and called out for Emma to buy their wares.

At a stand near the end of the market she found a wide-brimmed straw hat that would do, and a pair of Indian sandals not unlike the ones Miguel Rivas had worn yesterday.

She wondered about him. Although he had taken her to dinner, she did not think she would ever see him again. Strangely enough, she wasn't sure how she felt about that. He was an intriguing man, quite unlike anyone she had ever met. Though not football-player big and brawny, he was nevertheless overwhelmingly masculine. The first time he had spoken to her she had sensed a barely restrained strength and an almost hunterlike intentness that she had found both fascinating and frightening. It was the feeling that, in a way she could not explain, Miguel Rivas did not belong to the civilized world of superhighways, tall office buildings, computers, jet aircraft and satellite dishes; that instead he belonged to another, more primitive time. There was something about him that made her think of that carved stone figure of the God of Renewal.

Had he lived two thousand years ago, he might have been a priest. Or perhaps a warrior, one of the men who had defended the ancient city of Monte Alban against invaders, wearing only a loincloth to cover his nakedness, his body bronzed by the sun, his long legs... A flush of heat that had nothing to do with the weather colored her cheeks. What in the devil was wrong with her? Here she was, daydreaming about a man she would very likely never see again, a man who thought her father was a thief, and from the way he'd looked at her, that she was probably an accomplice to her father's supposed crimes.

She had heard stories about foreigners who had wound up in a Mexican jail, and for a moment last night Miguel Rivas had looked angry enough to have had her locked up. He was a macho Mexican with a mean gleam in his eye, and she wanted nothing to do with him.

On the other hand... She started across the street toward her hotel. On the other hand, if he really was an archaeologist, he could be of tremendous help. She was certainly curious to learn more about the newly discovered tomb. He had said the artifacts they'd found there were priceless. Information about the new tomb and the robbery attempts would add a great deal to the articles she wanted to write.

But she had no idea how she could get in touch with Rivas. When he had dropped her off last night, he hadn't asked to see her again. She was sorry about that now—only because he night be helpful in her research, of course.

Emma stopped at the desk to tell the clerk that she would be checking out. The phone rang. The clerk answered, then handed the phone to Emma.

"It is for you, Señorita Pilgrim," he said.

She took the phone with a nod of thanks and said, "Yes? Hello?"

"Señorita Pilgrim? *Buenos dias.* This is Miguel Rivas."

"Oh." She cleared her throat. "Good morning, Mr. Rivas."

"You said that you were writing a series of articles on the different archaeological sites in and around Oaxaca."

"Yes." Emma took a deep breath and crossed her fingers.

"I wonder if I could be of service to you. I'm driving out to Mitla this morning and I thought you might like to come along."

The day before yesterday she had made inquiries about how to get there. Twenty-five miles from Oaxaca, it would have been an expensive taxi ride, with no assurance that she could get a taxi back. This was a perfect opportunity, one she wouldn't pass up.

"I'd like to," she said, "but I'm moving out of the hotel this morning into an apartment."

"Then I'll help you move, and after that we will drive out to Mitla."

"Well, I—"

"I will wait for you at your hotel in half an hour. Is that sufficient time for you to get your things together?"

"Yes, but—"

"Half an hour then," he said, and hung up.

Emma stood there by the desk for a moment, trying to collect her thoughts. Then, with a shake of her head, she paid her bill and hurried up to her room to pack.

He told himself he had invited the North American woman to come with him to Mitla only so that he could keep an eye on her. That's what he intended doing, of course, but perhaps it was more than that. He had found her more interesting than any of the women he had currently been seeing. He liked her intelligence and the way she had stood up to him. And yes, he liked her understated, wholly natural look. At first glance he had thought her plain, but in the restaurant, with the candlelight adding a rosy glow to her skin and her wide green eyes looking so intently into his, he had found himself thinking how pretty she was. She intrigued him. He wanted to see more of her.

But, of course, that had nothing to do with his taking her to Mitla today.

When Miguel pulled the Jeep up in front of the hotel half an hour later, Emma was standing at the door next to her luggage and all of her photographic gear. She was wearing an apple green dress, sandals, and a wide-brimmed straw hat with matching ribbon tied round it. With her brown hair fashioned into a single thick braid down her back, she looked summer fresh and, yes, very pretty.

He took her to the apartment she had rented. It was small, shabby and unattractive. He carried her suitcase into the bedroom, noting the double bed with the blue chenille spread, the white dresser and the worn rug on the tile floor.

"Do you think you'll be comfortable here?" he asked doubtfully.

Emma shrugged. "It's only for a month or two," she said. "It will do."

"I'll wait if you'd like to unpack."

"No, I can do it later."

"Then we'd better get started. It's going to be hot today." He looked at his watch. It was almost noon. "You don't mind the heat?"

"Not too much. It gets hot in Denver in the summer, too."

"All right then, if you're sure." He led the way out to the Jeep and helped her in.

It was hot when they started out. The Jeep, unlike his car, wasn't air-conditioned; the air that blew in was as hot as a blast furnace.

It was almost one by the time they reached Mitla. Miguel parked under the shade of a pepper tree. Emma collected her camera and notebook and he took her camera case. The sun was high and bright. There was no breeze to cool the air.

"Most of what is here now dates back two or three centuries before the Spanish Conquest in 1521," Miguel told her as they started toward the Hall of Columns. "After the decline of Monte Alban, Mitla became one of the most important Zapotec centers in the area."

"It's different, though, isn't it? From Monte Alban, I mean." Emma stopped to look around. The sky was a pure, clear blue. The cream puff white clouds seemed to almost touch the distant mountains. Perhaps because of the heat there were only a few tourists out today, and it was almost as though she and Miguel Rivas were alone. And again, as she had in Monte Alban, she had the feeling that she was in a different time. And that he was quite unlike anyone she had ever known.

He wore jeans and a T-shirt, rather than the Indianlike clothes he'd worn the first time she had seen him. His shoulders were broader than she had thought, his hips narrow, his stomach flat, and his legs in the tight jeans were long and straight. Because she was uncomfortably aware of their solitude, Emma stepped away from him and began snapping pictures.

She photographed the Hall of Columns and the pre-Hispanic stone mosaics, stopping often to make notes. When she didn't understand something, Miguel explained it. He gave historical background and information with more patience than she had expected.

The heat became oppressive. She took her hat off and fanned her face, wishing she'd worn shorts instead of a dress. Her stomach felt just the least bit queasy, very likely because she hadn't had anything except tea that morning for breakfast.

She put her hat back on, and looking around with a shake of her head, said, "Where did they go, I wonder? What happened to them?"

"¿Quién sabe?" Miguel said. "Who knows? Originally Mitla was a Mixtec settlement. After the decline of Monte Alban, it became one of the most important Zapotec centers." He gazed out toward the mountains. "Perhaps illness decimated them. Perhaps they fled from warring tribes. It was not too different than our world today. One nation conquered another, then the Spanish came to conquer all of Mexico."

His face became impassive, his expression as inscrutable as those of the ancient gods. She thought that probably he was of Spanish as well as Indian blood, but it was the Indian blood that predominated, that made him the man he was. He might be polite, even pleasant, but she did not think anyone would ever see the man hidden behind the protective mask.

"Are you Zapotec or Mixtec?" she asked.

"Zapotec, with Spanish blood on my mother's side," he said. "There are nearly a million Indians in the state of Oaxaca, seventeen different peoples who make up a third of the state's population. We have different languages, different..." He stopped and looked more closely at Emma. "Your face is very red, Señorita Pilgrim. You'd better get out of the sun."

"Okay. Yes." The hard dry ground shimmered before her eyes. She had trouble focusing.

"We'd better get back to the Jeep."

Emma took a deep breath. "Maybe...maybe that's a good idea." She took a step. A sudden wave of dizziness made her stagger.

Miguel took her arm to steady her. "I've got a bottle of water in the Jeep," he said. "That will help." He put an arm around her waist.

She wanted to tell him it was just a momentary dizziness that would pass, but it seemed like such an effort to speak. She took a step. The ground rose and fell. The sun blinded her. Bright motes of dust swam before her eyes. She felt sick, strange....

He picked her up. She tried to protest, but he didn't listen as he ran toward the car. When he reached it he laid her down on a patch of grass under the pepper tree, then raised her head and held a bottle of water to her lips.

She took a few sips. "Feel sick," she managed to whisper.

He took her hat off, then wet his handkerchief and wiped her face. Her skin was hot and dry, and he knew he had to get her to a place that was cool. When he lifted her into the Jeep, she leaned her head back and closed her eyes.

He drove as fast as he could the few miles to the town of Mitla and pulled to a halt in front of a small hotel. She opened her eyes when they stopped, and didn't protest when he put an arm around her waist to help her out of the car.

She was vaguely aware of a shaded courtyard and a small lobby with a clean tile floor, and of the man at the reception desk who looked alarmed when he said, "*Ay, señor. ¿Qué pasa? ¿Su señora está enferma con el sol?*"

"Sí," Miguel said. "Do you have a room with a bathtub?"

"Sí, señor. And a ceiling fan." The man took a key from one of the slots behind him. "This way, *señor,*" he said, and hurried toward the hall to the right of the lobby.

"Listen," Emma tried to say. "I'm all right. I—"

Miguel scooped her up in his arms and followed the desk clerk. The room was large. The floor was tiled. He laid Emma on the bed while the other man connected the fan.

"If there is anything else, *señor,* anything at all, you need only to ask."

"Is there a doctor in town?"

"I'm afraid not."

"Then please bring a pitcher of water. And juice. Whatever you have."

"Certainly, sir." The man hurried out of the room and closed the door behind him.

Miguel ran into the bathroom. He turned the water on in the tub, then went back to Emma. She was semiconscious, her body temperature high, her skin hot and dry. He raised her up. "I'm going to undress you," he said.

Her eyelids fluttered. She managed a weak, "No," and tried to push him away.

"We've got to get you cooled off," he said. "That's the fastest way I know." He unbuttoned the top buttons of her dress and pulled it over her head.

She tried to shove his hands away. "Not right," she mumbled. "Taking advantage..."

When he had stripped her down to her bra and panties, he picked her up and carried her into the bathroom. The tub was half-full, the water cool. As gently as he could he laid her in it.

"Oh," she whispered, forgetting to be upset. "Oh, that's nice."

He knelt beside her and began to bathe her face. He cupped water into his hands and poured it over her head.

She lay back, eyes closed, and didn't object when he continued to bathe her face and hair. Her skin was still red and hot to the touch. The desk clerk knocked and came in with a pitcher of water and one of lemonade. Miguel had him put the pitchers on the floor beside him, and when the man left he filled a glass and held it to Emma's lips.

She took a sip, then opened her eyes and said, "Thank you."

"Take more."

"Yes." She drank half the glass. "I didn't have breakfast," she said. "Only tea. Maybe that's why I feel so... so rotten."

"You're not used to the sun. I should have known better than to have brought you here in the middle of the day."

"Not your fault. I..." She became aware that she was wearing only her bra and briefs, and that probably she should do something about covering herself or asking him to leave. She took another sip of juice while she thought about that. And finally, because it seemed like too much effort, she simply sank lower into the water and closed her eyes.

He felt her forehead, her arm, her ankle. He rested a hand on her shoulder. Her skin was cooler, but her face was still red. He continued bathing her face and squeezing water over her head. An hour passed. When her skin tones began to look more normal, he said, "Emma? How do you feel, Emma?"

"Better." Half-asleep, she nodded slightly.

He lifted her up out of the water. Before she could object, he had unfastened her bra and pulled her briefs down around her ankles.

"Hey!" She tried to push him away with hands as weak as a day-old pup.

He picked up a towel, ignoring her protests, and dried her off. Then he wrapped the towel around her hair and carried her into the other room, where he laid her on the bed beneath the ceiling fan. He pulled the sheet up to cover her nakedness and said, "Rest now. I'll be right here."

"That's what I'm afraid of," she mumbled. Then, with a sigh, she closed her eyes.

She slept for a little while. When she awakened, he held a glass of lemonade to her lips. She drank greedily, then took off the towel that bound her hair and lay back against the pillow. "I was having something like heatstroke, wasn't I?" she said.

"Something like that. Yes."

"Thank you for taking care of me. I'm sorry if I was difficult, but it's not every day a strange man undresses me and dunks me in a tub of cold water."

A corner of his mouth quirked in a smile. "It's not every day I undress a lady I don't know. Would you like something to eat? Soup and a salad, maybe?"

"Cold soup."

Miguel nodded. "I'll see what I can do. Will you be all right for a few minutes?"

"Yes, I'm feeling much better. Really."

He went out and she lay there looking up at the fan. She was feeling enough better to be embarrassed over having made a fool of herself. And to be overwhelmingly grateful to Miguel Rivas for taking care of her. He had been exceedingly kind, and although she knew little about it, she was sure he had done all of the right things. She felt better; still tired and weak, but better.

Miguel came back with a tray of food and a white cotton nightgown. "I borrowed this from one of the maids," he said when he handed it to her. "I thought you might enjoy your dinner more if you had something on."

Her face flushed from embarrassment, not from the heat.

"I'll wait in the bathroom while you change." He started toward the door, then, turning back, grinned and said, "Unless you need some help."

"No!" she said quickly, then, noting his grin, added, "I can manage."

The gown was clean and smelled of sunshine. Emma slipped it over her head, looking longingly at the tray of food, and called out, "You can come back now."

The gazpacho was cool. She ate a piece of home-made bread with it, and most of the fresh fruit salad.

"What time is it?" she asked when she finished. "We probably should be getting back to Oaxaca."

"It's seven-thirty," Miguel answered. "And no, we're not going back to Oaxaca tonight. The best thing you can do right now is to rest here where it's cool."

"What about you?" Emma raised an eyebrow. "Don't you have to get back?"

Miguel shook his head. "I'm going to stay here and keep an eye on you."

"Well..." Emma hesitated. "You don't mean here, as in this room."

"That's exactly what I mean."

"Really, Mr. Rivas—"

"Miguel," he said. "After the afternoon we've spent, I think first names are called for, don't you?"

Emma blushed again, and he found himself thinking that spending the night with her wasn't going to be such a chore after all.

She fussed and fumed about his staying in the same room with her. He went into the hotel dining room for a quick dinner, and when he returned she fussed and fumed some more.

He took his sandals off and pulled the T-shirt over his head. She looked at him, wide-eyed with indignation, and held the sheet up to her chin.

"If you think you're...you're going to..." She thrust her jaw out, too filled with indignation to go on.

"Make love to you?" He cocked one dark eyebrow. "My dear Emma," he said in a mocking voice, "you really should wait until you're asked."

She smacked her pillow and wished it were him.

"Don't worry," he said. "Young *gringa* tourists rarely appeal to me."

And grinned when she said, "Well!" and scooted over as far as she could to the other side of the bed.

He stretched out, arms under his head and sighed. "Good night, Emma Pilgrim," he said, and grinned again when she didn't answer.

Chapter 3

Emma awoke some time during the night. Too warm, she threw the sheet back, moving restlessly as she tried to find a cooler spot in the bed. She flung an arm out, and yelped when she touched Miguel's shoulder.

"What is it?" he asked, instantly awake. "Is anything wrong?"

"What are you doing here?" she cried before she'd woken up enough to remember that they were sleeping in the same bed.

He snapped on the bedside light. Her hair was tangled and the white nightgown was hitched up over her bare thighs. She looked delectably feminine. He averted his eyes, took a deep breath and asked, "What is it? Do you feel ill?"

Emma yanked the nightgown down. "Just awfully warm," she said. "And thirsty."

He got up and went to the dresser to pour her a glass of juice from the pitcher there. "This will help," he said when he brought it to her. He put his hand on her forehead. She was warm, but nothing like she'd been that afternoon.

"Do you feel well enough to get into the shower? It would help cool you off."

She looked up at him over the rim of her glass, her eyes sleepy, her mouth softly vulnerable. The defenses of the day before were down. She still wasn't happy about his being here with her, but she seemed to have accepted him. She took another sip of the juice and wiped her mouth with the back of her hand.

"A shower would feel good," she said, and started to swing her feet off her side of the bed.

But before she could, Miguel said, *"Momento,"* and hurried around to help her. "Stand up slowly," he cautioned. "Make sure you're all right."

"It's okay." Emma looked up at him. "I'm not going to faint or anything."

He put an arm around her waist and walked her to the bathroom door. "Sure you can manage?" he asked.

Her legs were wobbly, but because she was afraid he'd offer to come into the shower with her if she told him that, she said a hasty, "Yes, thank you," and went in and closed the door. Then she quickly pulled the gown over her head and got into the shower.

The water was blessedly cool. She lifted her hair off her shoulders, and with her eyes closed, let the wet coolness run down her body. She felt infinitely better than she had yesterday. Still a little shaky, but the terrible sickness, the feeling of helplessness and confusion, had dissipated. Though she felt awkward and more than a little uncomfortable about Miguel Rivas sleeping in the same bed with her, she understood that he'd been concerned and wanted to keep an eye on her.

Finally, after almost ten minutes, Emma turned the water off and stepped out of the shower. It was then she saw her panties and bra hanging over a towel rack.

"Oh God!" she sputtered, remembering that he had stripped her naked and dried her off. There wasn't anything to do about it now; he had done what he had to, and hopefully he was gentleman enough to never mention it.

Her face was still a little flushed and her hair was a mess. She looked at herself in the mirror and shook her head. When she had put the gown on she opened the door and said, "Would you give me my purse, please?"

"Hold on." Miguel crossed the room and picked it up off the chair. "Here you are," he said, and handed it to her.

"Thank you." Emma closed the door, then pulled her hairbrush out of the bag and began trying to work the tangles out of her hair. When it was smooth and straight, she glanced in the mirror, and shook her head again because she still looked a little the worse for wear.

Miguel had been standing by the window gazing out into the night, but he turned when he heard her come out of the bathroom.

"Well, that's better," she said. "I feel . . ." She stopped. His sleek black hair was tousled from sleep. He was barefoot and bare chested, and his body, bronzed by the sun and by his Zapotec ancestry, was clean and pure of line. His face had an aesthetic look that made her think of a Spanish priest of the Inquisition, or of an ancient Zapotec god. Yes, she thought, if ancient gods wore blue jeans, Miguel Rivas would surely have been a god.

He said, "More juice?" and she stared at him, still lost in thought.

"Would you like more juice?" he asked.

"Uh, yes." She shook her head to clear away the vision of him, or the him that might have lived a thousand years ago. "Some juice. Yes. Thanks."

He looked puzzled as he handed her the glass.

"What time is it?" she asked.

"A little after three. Do you feel all right?"

Emma nodded. "I'm sorry to have been such a nuisance. I haven't thanked you properly for taking care of me. And I do—thank you, I mean. You've been very kind."

Miguel shook his head. "It was my fault it happened. I should have known better than to have taken you out in the middle of the day when you're not used to the heat. The next time we'll get an early start."

The next time? Emma felt a sudden flare of excitement. In spite of all the trouble she'd caused him, he was still willing to show her around the archaeological sites. She was pleased, and not just because he was an archaeologist who could be helpful.

She finished the juice and put the empty glass back on the dresser.

"We'd better get to bed," Miguel said.

"Yes." But still Emma stood there, a little embarrassed, a little confused.

In the circle of light her body, through the sheerness of the white cotton gown, was clearly defined. This time Miguel didn't avert his eyes. He drank in every inch of her, the straight brown hair that streamed softly down over her shoulders, the wide green eyes that looked into his, the vulnerable mouth, the sweet rounded lines of her body. Desire flamed through him. He said, "Emma?"

Small white teeth clamped her lower lip. Her arms came up to cover her chest.

He took a step toward her, then stopped. "You— you'd better get back to bed. I'm going to go outside, get some air, check on the Jeep." He switched off the light and headed for the door. "Try to get some sleep," he said. And as though the devil himself were after him, he went out and closed the door.

Emma stood in the darkness in the middle of the room. Except for the whir of the overhead fan, everything was quiet. The room felt strangely empty without him. From somewhere near the building she heard a dog bark, then Miguel's voice, speaking low and reassuringly in Spanish.

A sigh quivered through her. She went slowly to the bed and lay down. She closed her eyes and saw once again the desire in his, a desire that had both frightened and excited her.

"Ridiculous," she said aloud. Then a slight smile curved her lips.

In a little while she went to sleep, and did not awaken when Miguel finally came in and lay down beside her.

He was gone when she awoke the next morning, but there was a note propped up on the dresser that read, "I'm having breakfast in the patio."

She showered again, then brushed and braided her hair and dressed. She felt stronger now, and hungry.

He was in the patio, seated at a round table under a blooming poinciana tree. He got up as soon as he saw her, smiled and pulled out a chair for her.

"Good morning," he said. "You look much better."

Emma nodded. "Yes, I'm fine. And hungry. I guess that's a good sign."

"I'm sure it is." He signaled the waiter. "What will you have?" he asked Emma.

"Everything!" she said with a laugh. And ordered ham and eggs and orange juice.

The fresh orange juice came in a tall glass, the ham and eggs with refried beans, cheese and tortillas. Emma ate half of everything that was on her plate, then leaned back to catch her breath and look around. The patio was small but pretty and green. Gardenia bushes flourished. There were wild orchids, bright red hibiscus and tiger lilies. Purple bougainvillea covered one wall. A cup-of-gold vine climbed another.

"It's lovely here," she said.

Miguel nodded. "That's one of the few advantages of a hot climate. We have a lot of flowers." He looked at her. "How do you feel this morning?"

"I'm fine now, thanks to you."

Her color was good, but he had a feeling she was still a little shaky. "You should rest a day or two when you get back to your apartment," he said. "Don't try to do too much of anything."

Emma started to object, to tell him that she was perfectly okay. But she didn't. Miguel was probably right. This was his country; he knew it better than she did. "I'd like to come back to Mitla again," she said. "I felt so rotten yesterday that I really didn't get a chance to look at everything I wanted to."

"I need to come back, too." Miguel took a sip of his coffee. "We could see Dainzu and Lambityeco on another day."

"I don't want to interfere with your work." Emma hesitated. "Or with your personal life. I mean, if you have a family," she finished.

"I have two children."

"Oh." She managed a smile. "How nice," she murmured.

"Angelina is three and Jose Antonio is five."

"Well." She took a bite of her scrambled eggs while she tried to think of something to say. But all she could come up with was, "Cute ages."

"I suppose." He put his coffee cup down. "Their mother is dead," he said. "The children live with my mother in Dos Santos, a village forty miles from Oaxaca."

"Do you see them often?"

"Not as often as I should."

Why? she wondered, but didn't ask.

They finished the rest of their breakfast in silence. Miguel looked troubled; she was thoughtful. When it was time to leave the hotel she said, "It's because of me we had to stay here," and handed her credit card to the man behind the desk.

"I'm sorry, *señorita*," the man apologized. "But we are a small hotel and do not take credit cards."

Miguel paid in cash, and only smiled when Emma said, "I'll pay you back as soon as we get to Oaxaca."

They left at nine. By then the temperature was already in the nineties.

"Next time I'll take the car," Miguel said. "It's air-conditioned."

The next time. Emma settled back against the seat and smiled.

The day after her return from Mitla, Emma went shopping again in the market. She bought a few pieces of green pottery, several big bright Mexican paper flowers, a papier-mâché clown, plants, and a colorful pillow for the sofa. This was going to be her nest for a few weeks, and she wanted to make it livable.

When that was done she arranged the darkroom more to her liking, and developed the photographs she had taken at Monte Alban and Mitla.

The few that she had snapped in Mitla were fair, but the photos she had taken at Monte Alban were sensational. There hadn't been anyone around that stormy day. In the pictures the dark clouds hung low and threateningly ominous over the crumbling ruins of the deserted city.

This is what it had been like in those long-ago days before the Spanish came, she thought. It would have been as quiet as this on such a day, just before a storm. Where had they gone, she wondered yet again, the men and women who had lived in this ancient city? And why?

In a way she could not explain, it seemed to her as she gazed at the photographs that time turned back and that she was actually seeing Monte Alban as it had been so long ago. For a moment she felt an almost overwhelming sadness for those people who had lived in this ancient place.

With a sigh, telling herself that she was being foolishly sentimental, she put the last picture she had taken into the developing fluid. Slowly, slowly, like a ghostly temple from the past, the pyramid shimmered in the chemicals. Then it emerged, the top half of it lost in the clouds. And through the clouds the figure of Miguel Rivas descended like a god of old down from the heavens.

"The cloud man," she said under her breath, and knew that was the way she would always think of him. For though he was a modern man, an educated man, there was a part of him that seemed not to belong in the modern world, a part of him that surely came from another, older civilization.

Three days had passed since they had been at Mitla. She had not heard from him. Now, as she hung the photo alongside the others, she wondered if she would. And knew that if she didn't, she would be bitterly disappointed.

But the next morning while she was having breakfast, someone knocked at her door. And when she opened it, a short balding man with a sad, drooping mustache bowed and said in very bad English, "The Señor Rivas ask me to this note give it to you. Yes?"

"Yes," Emma said.

"*Y contestar,* please yes?"

¿Contestar? Emma thought for a moment. "Answer," she said. "Yes, I will answer." She motioned the man inside and opened the note.

"Would you like to have dinner with me tonight?" Miguel had written. "Seven-thirty?"

"Momento," she told the man, and taking a piece of paper from the small table under the windows, wrote, "Yes, thank you. Seven-thirty is fine."

That afternoon she tried to take a nap. She lay flat on the not-too-comfortable bed with her feet elevated, and cold tea bags over her eyes, because she'd read somewhere that doing so made your eyes look brighter. But an hour later, when she peered into the mirror, her eyes looked exactly as they had before.

She took a leisurely bath in the claw-footed tub, washed her hair, and when it was dry, brushed it until it was smooth and silky. After that she polished her nails, not quite sure why she was going to all this trouble or why the thought of seeing Miguel Rivas again excited her.

For the first time in a long time she put on eye makeup and lipstick. At seven she stepped into a sleeveless black dress that did nice things for her figure, sheer black stockings and high-heeled pumps that showed off her fairly elegant legs. Then perfume—a drop behind each ear, the hollow of her throat, her wrists.

The apartment, even with its ceiling fans and cross ventilation, was hot. So was she. And nervous. By seven thirty-five she was convinced Miguel wasn't coming. Five minutes later he knocked on her door.

He had on a white suit with a black shirt, and he was every bit as good-looking as she remembered. "Black and white," he said, as he handed her a bouquet of pink roses. "We go well together, yes?"

Yes indeedy, Emma thought, but because her heart was beating a tom-tom rhythm in her chest, she only nodded and said, "Thank you for the roses. They're lovely," and headed into the kitchen to find something to put them in.

"How are you feeling?" he asked.

"Perfectly fine." She came back into the living room, the flowers in a pretty clay pitcher. She put them on the coffee table in front of the wicker sofa and stood back to admire them. "They make the place seem homier," she said.

The room seemed less shabby, pleasant and warm now that Emma had a few things of her own in it. He smiled at the papier-mâché clown in an orange shirt and blue-and-green-striped overalls. Next to the clown there was a small flowering plant and a beautifully colored abalone shell. A leafy green fern had been placed near the windows, and books had been arranged on the table near the fern.

Emma leaned forward to adjust the roses, and the fall of her hair brushed her cheek. She isn't just pretty, Miguel thought suddenly. She's so much more than that. There was an elegance about her, a fineness of bone structure and carriage that told of class and breeding. Her eyes, as green as the new leaves of the laurel trees, were wide set and beautiful. Her nose was straight, her mouth well shaped and generous. She was a lovely woman, a woman he wanted to know better.

He looked at the books she had arranged in a small bookcase. There were two volumes of poetry, a new Ludlum, Gabriel García Marquez's *Love in the Time of Cholera*, Prescott's *Conquest of Mexico*, Calde-

ron's *Life in Mexico,* an intermediate Spanish text-
book and a Spanish dictionary.

"Have you been doing your homework?" he asked
with a smile.

Emma smiled back, more at ease now. "I really
want to learn the language," she said. "I can get by
well enough, but I'd like to be better than that."

"Stay longer and you will." His mouth quirked and
there was something in his eyes she couldn't quite read.
"I guarantee it."

"I . . ." The room seemed to be getting warmer by
the minute. "I wish I could," she said, "but I'm a
working girl, not a lady of leisure." She hesitated.
"Speaking of work, would you like to see the pictures
I took that day at Monte Alban?"

"Yes, of course."

"There aren't many of them. I hadn't really planned
to take any that day, but then the storm came and
everything suddenly got so still and beautiful and
mysterious looking, I couldn't resist. Wait a moment
and I'll get them."

When she came back she laid the half-dozen photos on the kitchen table.

Because she was a professional, Miguel had expected her to be good. But she was more than that. She
had somehow managed to capture the mystery that
was Monte Alban. Perhaps it was the somberness of
the dark clouds, perhaps the grayness of the sky, but
this *gringa,* this woman who had never been here before, had somehow been able to catch the essence of
the ancient city.

He turned away from the photographs to look at her. Her lower lip was clamped between her teeth. Her eyes were anxious, waiting for his approval.

"They're wonderful, Emma," he said softly. "Wonderful."

She let out the breath she didn't even know she'd been holding. "This is the last," she said, and turned over the photograph of the pyramid.

"You looked as though you were coming out of the clouds," she said shyly. "The first time I saw you...like this...I thought you were one of those ancient gods come out of the clouds to become man. I thought..." She raised her eyes to his, embarrassed, unable to go on.

Miguel rested his hands on her shoulders. "I'm not a god, Emma. I'm a man."

Her eyes widened and he saw an awareness come into them, an awareness of him. He tightened his hands on her shoulders. He whispered her name, "Emma?" and before she could step away, he drew her into his arms and kissed her.

She gave a small gasp of surprise before her lips softened and her arms came up to hold him as he held her.

It was a breathless kiss, shy at first, then warm and lingering, and surely more intense than he had intended it to be.

"Let her go," a voice inside his head whispered. But this was no time for listening to voices, not when his body was so alive, not when the blood was thrumming hot through his veins. *Dios!* He had not felt like this in years. Why now? Why with this one particular woman?

Without conscious thought he slid one hand down to the small of her back to draw her tightly against him, and when he felt her body hot against his, he murmured low in his throat, a growl-like sound in the silence of the room.

"Please—" she tried to say. But he took her words and kissed her, his mouth hard on hers, his tongue thrusting past her parted lips to find and touch her tongue.

She answered his kiss, but only for a moment. "Let me go," she whispered.

He tightened his arms around her. He felt the delicacy of her bones, the smoothness of her skin, and pressed her closer. He wanted to pick her up and carry her into the bedroom. He wanted—

"Miguel..." A whispered plea. "Miguel, please."

He stepped away from her.

Her eyes were luminous, her lips full and tremulous. She took a shuddering breath and he saw the rise and fall of her breasts. He took a step toward her, then stopped.

"I don't usually behave this way," he said. "I apologize. I hope you'll forgive me. Shall we go or would you rather not?"

"Go?"

"To dinner. If you still want to. If you're not angry."

"I'm not..." Emma shook her head. "I don't know what I am. I..." She lifted her shoulders, then the barest suggestion of a smile softened her mouth. "Yes, I do," she said. "I'm hungry."

She turned away to pick up her purse, and he saw that her hands were trembling.

He opened the door, and as she stepped through he put a detaining hand on her arm. She looked up at him, and because he couldn't help himself, he cupped her face in his hands and kissed her again, this time softly, gently.

"I'm sorry," he said when he let her go. "Not that I kissed you, but that I might have upset you."

"I—I'm not upset, Miguel."

The suggestion of a smile softened his face. "I like the way you say my name. Say it again and we'll go."

She looked up at him quizzically. "Miguel?"

"Yes," he said, "like that." Then he took her hand and they left.

Chapter 4

The restaurant Miguel took her to had an upstairs patio overlooking the beautiful old town square. On the south side of the square was the Governor's Palace; the cathedral stood at the north side. No cars were allowed in the *zocalo,* where colorful stands displayed blankets and rugs, black pottery, serapes and embroidered Mayan dresses, painted wooden animals, handwoven belts, reed baskets, clay pots and Mickey Mouse balloons.

Young couples strolled arm in arm. Pregnant ladies sat fanning themselves on the iron benches, while small children played near the fountain.

Miguel ordered salad and steak and red wine, and though he did not speak about what had passed between them earlier, it was all Emma could think about every time she looked at him.

At twenty-five she had dated her share of men, yet tonight when Miguel Rivas had kissed her she had felt something very special. It had left her wanting more.

Again and again as the evening progressed she found herself stealing glances at him, and wondering if the kisses they had shared had affected him the way they had her. If they had, he gave no indication of it.

After dinner, as they walked around the *zocalo,* he reached for her hand. A band was playing in the center kiosk, children splashed water in the fountain, and when a woman approached them offering gardenias, Miguel bought Emma a small bouquet.

When she thanked him, he only smiled and said, "A woman like you should always have flowers." Then, taking her hand again, he said, "Would you like to go to Dainzu tomorrow? I should see the children, and Dos Santos is on the way. I thought we might stop there first, if you wouldn't mind."

"No." Emma looked up at him. "I'd like to."

"Is seven too early? We could have breakfast at my mother's."

"Seven is fine." She looked at a boy and girl standing in front of the bench across from them. The little boy was blowing bubbles through a bubble pipe and the girl, younger than he, was laughing as the bubbles drifted above her. The young mother laughed, too, and suddenly Emma found herself wondering what Miguel's children were like. And about their mother. The woman he had loved.

In a little while they went back to the car. He helped her in, but he was silent on the drive back to her apartment. His face in the dim light of the dashboard looked remote, his expression unreadable. Would he kiss her again? Emma wondered with a tingle of anticipation mixed with confusion. Part of her was afraid he would and part was afraid he wouldn't, and still another part considered what if, because he had kissed her and because she had responded, he expected more.

When they arrived she would offer her hand, she decided, thank him for a nice evening and make a quick exit. If he tried to come in she would tell him politely but firmly that she did not believe in casual relationships. He had behaved like a gentleman before, so surely he would accept her refusal gracefully. And after all, it was up to the woman to set the rules in a relationship. Wasn't it?

By the time Miguel parked the car and came around to help her out, Emma was absolutely sure she was in control. He walked her to her door. "I'll see you safely inside," he said.

"That's not necessary."

"Please." He held his hand out for her key and she handed it to him.

He unlocked the door.

"Listen..." she started to say, just as he gave the key back to her.

"Good night, Emma," he said. "Thank you for having dinner with me. I'll see you in the morning. Sleep well."

"Yes, you...uh, you, too."

Then he was gone, leaving her alone with her polite words of refusal silent on her lips.

Maria Leticia Vargas de Rivas was a tall spare woman in her middle fifties. Her skin was of a darker color than her son's, but her cheekbones were the same and so were her dark eyes. She looked even more Indian than Miguel, but perhaps, Emma thought, that was because of the long black skirt and black, high-necked blouse she wore without an adornment of any kind.

She met them at the door of the adobe ranch house, which was set well off the road. A high stone fence surrounded the property, and though the land around the house was pretty and green, there was a feeling of grim remoteness about the place that made Emma uncomfortable even before his mother greeted her.

"I speak no English," Maria Leticia said in a coolly imperious voice when Miguel introduced them. "If we are to speak it must be in Spanish."

Great, Emma thought, for though she understood a lot of the language, her own vocabulary was fairly limited.

She made herself smile, then the smile became real when she saw the little girl peeping from behind the sofa. Big dark eyes that looked almost too large for her face were fringed by long lashes. Two skinny braids hung over her shoulders. A little boy who looked like a miniature Miguel stood next to her.

"*¿Papá?*" the boy said.

Maria Leticia turned to the children. "Come and greet your father and his guest," she ordered. "Quickly now. Don't just stand there."

The boy put a hand on his sister's shoulder and together they crossed the living room toward their father.

"Hola," Miguel said. He gave the boy a brief hug, then picked up the little girl and kissed her. *"¿Como están? ¿Bien?"*

"Sí, Papá," the boy said.

"This is Señorita Emma Pilgrim," Miguel told the boy and girl. "She's from the United States. Emma, these are my children, Jose Antonio and Angelina."

Jose Antonio offered Emma his hand. *"Mucho gusto,"* he said.

"Mucho gusto, Jose Antonio."

Miguel set the little girl down. "Say hello to Señorita Pilgrim," he prompted.

Angelina put her thumb in her mouth and looked up at Emma, her face solemn, her manner subdued.

"How do you do?" Emma said, but the little girl only ducked her head.

"Take your thumb out of your mouth." Maria Leticia frowned at the little girl. *"De veras,* in truth, Miguel I don't know what to do about the child. I've done everything I can think of to stop her from sucking her thumb. Last week I rubbed it with a chili and made her suck it."

"A chili?" Emma hadn't understood every word, but knew enough to be certain the woman was talking about putting chili on little Angelina's thumb. "But . . ." She started to protest, then stopped.

"She really cried," Jose Antonio said.

"Mother . . ." Miguel hesitated, then with a frown said, "I wish you wouldn't do that. Angelina is only three. She—"

"Needs to learn," Maria Leticia finished. "You've given me the responsibility of raising your children, Miguel. I wish you wouldn't interfere. Now come,

Hortensia has prepared breakfast and it's ready." She turned to Emma. "We're having a typical Mexican breakfast, *señorita*. I hope you don't mind."

"On the contrary," Emma responded. "I'm quite fond of Mexican food."

"I thought all Americans ate bran and yogurt for breakfast."

Emma gritted her teeth and forced a smile. "Not all Americans, *señora*."

Miguel put an arm around her waist and led her into the kitchen. Colorful clay pots and straw flowers adorned one side of the adobe walls, and floor-to-ceiling shelves were lined with blue-and-white dishes. It was far more cheerful than the lackluster living room had been.

"This is Hortensia," Miguel said, and an Indian woman in her late twenties, dressed in a bright flowered skirt, a white blouse and huaraches, turned from the modern stove to smile at Emma.

"*Buenos dias,* Señor Rivas," she said. "It is good to see you. You are hungry, *sí?*"

"*¡Sí!*" Miguel smiled. "This is Miss Pilgrim, Hortensia. And very likely she's as hungry as I am."

"Then you eat good, yes?" The Indian woman winked at Emma. "I fix eggs with chorizos, frijoles and *chilaquiles*."

"I'd better warn you about Hortensia's *chilaquiles*," Miguel said. "They're hot as—"

"As hot as love," Hortensia finished with a laugh.

"Hortensia!" Maria Leticia's face darkened. "Mind your manners!"

"She didn't mean anything, Mother." Miguel held a chair for Emma, then lifted Angelina onto the chair next to him and tucked a napkin under her chin. "Hortensia's almost a part of the family," he told Emma, ignoring his mother's remark. "We couldn't manage without her."

Mouth tight as a strung bow, Maria Leticia sat next to Jose Antonio.

The food was good, the conversation stilted. Miguel asked Jose Antonio how he liked going to kindergarten, but before the boy could answer, Maria Leticia said, "I decided he should wait and start first grade in the fall."

"But we discussed this, Mother. Jose said he wanted to go to school and we agreed that he should. He needs to be prepared to enter the first grade."

"He is prepared, probably better than the children who attend *kinder.* I give him his lessons every morning and afternoon. He knows the alphabet, he can read and write simple words and add simple figures."

"That's wonderful, and I'm sure you're doing an excellent job. But Jose needs to be with other children, boys and girls of his own age."

Very carefully, Maria Leticia placed her knife and fork across her plate. "If you do not like the way I am raising your children—"

"*¡Por Dios!* I didn't say that. I only said we had agreed that this summer he would start school. Why must you . . ."

Emma glanced at the two children. Jose Antonio, his fork halfway to his mouth, looked from his father to his grandmother, his dark eyes anxious. But little Angelina slipped farther down in her chair, head lowered, thumb in her mouth, her breakfast almost untouched.

"Sit up straight!" Maria Leticia frowned at her granddaughter. "And stop acting like a baby."

But she is a baby, Emma wanted to say. Appetite gone, she pushed the food around on her plate and pretended to eat. Miguel's face was grim; the children were silent. Only Maria Leticia's voice was heard, ordering Hortensia to pour more coffee and to bring more tortillas.

And just as Hortensia did, just as she put them on the table, Angelina reached for her glass of milk. They bumped and the glass of milk overturned.

"Now look what you've done!" Miguel's mother slapped the small hand. "Go to your room at once."

Angelina burst into tears. Miguel shoved his chair back, picked the child up and held her close. "Don't cry, little one," he said, and kissed the hand his mother had slapped.

"Really, Miguel!" Maria Leticia threw her napkin down on the table. "How do you expect her to learn any manners if you overrule everything I do?"

"We've talked about this before," he said angrily. "I won't have the children abused."

"Abused? A slap on the hand is abuse? Don't be ridiculous."

He tightened his arms around Angelina, kissed her, then set her down and said, "If you've finished your breakfast, why don't you go to your room like Grandmother said."

Angelina's lower lip trembled, but with a sniff she turned and left the kitchen.

Emma, who wanted to shake both Miguel and his mother, lost her appetite. She refused the basket of *pan dulce,* the sweet bread that was offered, and afraid she would say something she shouldn't, asked to be excused.

"The bathroom is through the living room and down the hall to the right," Miguel said. "Would you like Hortensia to show you the way?"

Emma shook her head. "I can find it." She shoved her chair back and without even an "Excuse me," left the room.

When she was a little girl and had been angry, she'd stomped her feet. Every time her father had said, "Emma, go to your room!" she'd stomped her way up the stairs, only to be told to come back down and climb the stairs properly.

But Angelina hadn't stomped, she'd slipped away as silently as a small ghost, head down, the ever-present thumb in her mouth.

Emma herself didn't stomp, but she did vent some of her anger by banging the bathroom door. Okay, she told herself when she was alone. Okay, okay, okay. Miguel is a widower doing the best he can. And so, probably, is his mother. It can't be easy coping with two small children. You'd be cross sometimes, too, if you had a three- and a five-year-old to take care of all day.

Cross, maybe, but not cottonmouth mean.

She splashed cold water over her face and brushed her hair, lingering in the bathroom because she didn't want to have to face the Mexican dragon lady just yet.

As she started down the hall, she heard the sound of crying and knew that it was Angelina. She hesitated. This isn't your business, she told herself sternly. This is between Miguel and his mother and his children. You're an outsider. It isn't your affair.

That's what she told herself even as she hurried toward the sound of the crying.

The little girl lay facedown on the bed, a fuzzy, lop-eared toy dog clutched in one arm.

"Angelina?" Emma took a step into the room. "*¿Niña?* Little girl?"

The child turned a tear-streaked face and tried to stifle a sob.

Emma took another step into the room. "Baby," she said. "Oh, baby." In two strides she reached the bed and gathered Angelina into her arms. "Don't cry, sweetie," she whispered, and began to rock the child back and forth in her arms.

At first the little body stiffened, then the arms crept up around Emma's neck. Emma felt the wetness of tears against her face and the small shudders that ran through the slight body.

"It's all right, baby," she said in English, knowing that even though Angelina couldn't understand the words, she would understand the tenderness. "Don't cry, sweetheart. Everything's going to be all right."

"*Mi papá está enojado,* my daddy is mad," Angelina whispered.

"No, he isn't. *Tu papá* loves... *amo* ..." Was that the word? "Your *papá* loves you, Angelina. *De veras,* truly, dear."

"But I..." Then words that Emma couldn't understand. But she caught the word *leche* and knew that Angelina was telling her that her grandmother and *papá* were both angry because she had spilled her milk.

"All little boys and girls spill their milk once in a while," Emma said in stumbling Spanish. "Sometimes even big people do."

She settled Angelina onto her lap and put a finger under her chin. "I'm sure your father and your grandmother love you very much."

"I have to stay in my room," Angelina whispered.

And a bare and tasteless room it is, Emma thought. A single bed with a brown bedspread. Brown drapes at the window; a chair, a dresser. A shelf filled with toys and dolls that looked as though they hadn't been touched.

"You have your toys and your dolls to play with, though." Emma pointed to a doll whose yellow hair had been frizzed up onto the top of her head. "She's pretty," she said. "Would you like to play with her?"

"I can't. Grandma said I spoiled her hair so I can't play with her anymore."

"Well..." Wanting to gnash her teeth, Emma tugged on the ear of the lop-eared dog. "What's his name?" she asked.

"Cisco."

"What kind of a dog is he?"

"A boy dog."

Emma patted his head. "Hi, Cisco," she said.

Angelina chuckled, then shyly touched Emma's hair. "*Bonito,*" she said shyly. "Your hair is *muy bonito.*"

"Yes," Miguel said from the doorway. "It is." He came into the room. "I wondered where you were," he said to Emma.

"I heard Angelina crying." Her mouth tightened. "She was very upset."

"I'm sorry. Mother isn't feeling well. She has a migraine."

She *is* a migraine, Emma wanted to say. Instead she said, "They can be nasty."

"Yes." He avoided her eyes. "I think we should be going now." He reached down to take Angelina off Emma's lap. "Don't cry any more, *querida,*" he said. "Grandma's not mad. She was just a little upset that you spilled your milk. Would you like another glass?"

Angelina shook her head.

"Would you like to come out to the car and say goodbye to me and to Miss Pilgrim?"

Angelina nodded, and when he put her down she reached for Emma's hand.

Jose Antonio was waiting for them next to the car. "Where are you going?" he asked.

"To the ruins at Dainzu," Miguel answered.

"Can I go?"

"I'm afraid not this time, Jose." And when the boy's face fell, Miguel said, "Maybe next time."

"We could have a picnic," Emma said. "Un peek-neek."

The children looked at her, not understanding.

"Un dia de campo," Miguel translated. "Would you like that?"

"Yes!" Jose Antonio said. "Can we, *Papá?* Can we?"

Miguel looked at his children. Emma waited. "Yes," he said. "I have to go to Mexico City in a few days, but we can do it as soon as I return. We'll make a whole day of it." He ruffled Jose's hair. "All right?"

"¡Sí, Papá!" The little boy was all but jumping up and down with excitement, and for a moment at least, Angelina took her thumb out of her mouth.

"Jose Antonio has his lessons in the morning," Maria Leticia said from the front steps of the house.

"Missing one day won't hurt him." Miguel crossed to where she stood. *"Adiós, Mamá,"* he said. "Thank you for the breakfast. It was delicious."

"Yes." Emma offered her hand. "Thank you."

Maria Leticia nodded. "When will you be returning to the United States, Señorita Pilgrim?" she said.

And instead of saying that she would be returning in five or six weeks, Emma smiled and shrugged. "I really have no idea," she said. "I suppose it depends..." She let that hang in the air for a moment or two, then to Miguel said, "It's going to be hot soon. I think we'd better go."

"Yes, we want to get there as early as we can." He picked Angelina up, kissed both her cheeks and said, "I'll see you soon. Be a good girl and mind your grandmother."

And when he put her down, Emma said, *"Adiós, Angelina. Hasta pronto.* She took the little girl's thumb out of her mouth and kissed it, and in English said, "Bye-bye, sweetie."

"Bye-bye," Angelina whispered.

Then Jose Antonio shook hands with her and Miguel opened the door on her side of the car.

"Adiós," he called out as they drove away. And to Emma he said, "This is always the hardest part about coming. I hate to leave them."

"How often do you see them?"

"Not as often as I should."

"Why?"

He frowned and she knew that she had been too forward. And as long as she had... She cleared her throat. "Your mother is awfully strict with them, isn't she?"

The frown deepened. "She's raising them the same way she raised me, and I turned out well enough." He shot Emma a look. "Education begins in the home," he said. "Children need discipline and control."

"And love? What about love?"

He sent her another glance and she saw the anger in his eyes. "My mother loves my children, as I do," he said. "They come first in my life and they always will." His mouth tightened. "Perhaps if you had children of your own you would better understand the problem of raising them."

Emma lifted her chin and glared back at him. "Perhaps," she said. "And perhaps I'd make a lousy mother. But one thing I know for sure, I wouldn't smack a kid for spilling her milk."

And with that she looked straight ahead, as did he, and neither of them spoke until they reached the ruins of Dainzu.

Chapter 5

Miguel had married Yolanda Torres when he was seventeen and she was sixteen. She was the first girl he had ever been intimate with, and they had married because she had thought she was pregnant. The idea of marriage had scared the hell out of him, but he'd had no choice in the matter. Yolanda's father had demanded he do the right thing and he had.

His mother had called Yolanda a *puta,* and when he had defended the girl, Maria Leticia had slapped him across his face.

He and Yolanda had been married in the parish church, and at his mother's insistence, they had moved in with his parents. That had been a mistake; both he and Yolanda had been miserably unhappy. A week after the wedding, Yolanda had discovered that she wasn't pregnant after all. It was then he had decided, over her tearful protestations that she would surely go to hell, that they would use birth control.

He'd finished *preparatorio,* and with a part-time job and the help of his father, had managed to put himself through the University of Oaxaca. By this time he knew that he wanted to be an archaeologist, and that he would do whatever he had to to accomplish his goal. He applied for and received a scholarship to the University of Mexico in Mexico City. There he took another part-time job and found a small apartment for himself and Yolanda. But when he asked her to come to Mexico City, she refused.

"I can't leave my family," she had said.

"But you and I are a family," he'd told her. "You're my wife. I want you to be with me."

But she had been adamant, and Miguel had gone off to Mexico City alone. He went home as often as he could, but never once in the two years he was there did Yolanda come to visit him.

Though they were separated, he had remained faithful to her, not so much out of a sense of obligation as the fact that between his job in a clothing factory and his university studies he was too tired to look for a girl, much less become involved in a distracting relationship.

His father died during his first year in Mexico City and Miguel went home for the funeral. He and Yolanda spent a week together, and it had been like being with a stranger.

His mother had come to his graduation, but Yolanda had not. With a degree in archaeology in his hand and the promise of a job with the Department of

Antiquities, he'd returned to Oaxaca, where he rented an apartment for himself and Yolanda.

Yolanda became pregnant. She was a good mother. Jose Antonio was a healthy, happy baby, and they got along well enough. Two years after their son was born, Yolanda once again became pregnant.

She was seven and a half months along when the department Miguel worked for sent him to Honduras to assist the government there in the excavation of a recently discovered site. It was a wonderful opportunity for him, and because he'd known it would further his career, and because they said he could return when it was time for his wife to deliver, he had accepted.

Three weeks into the job, he had received a call from his mother. Yolanda had been rushed to the hospital; the baby had arrived early, the doctors were worried. He'd taken the first flight out of Tegucigalpa. His mother met him at the airport with the news that Yolanda was dead and that he had a baby daughter.

He had been consumed with guilt because he had left Yolanda. And because he knew in his heart that he had never loved his wife.

He hired a nurse to take care of Jose Antonio and the baby, Angelina. After the first month the nurse quit and his mother came from Dos Santos to take care of the children.

After that he tried a series of combination housekeeper-nursemaids, and twice a week his mother came to the city to supervise and make sure everything was all right. But none of the housekeepers had worked out, and when his mother told him it would be better for the children if she took care of them herself, he had agreed.

He knew that she was rigid in her ideas of child raising, but he also knew that his mother loved Jose Antonio and Angelina. He had done his best not to interfere.

Now here was this *gringa,* this outsider, suggesting that his mother was too strict. She'd never had children. How could she know the difficulties of raising them? She had no business criticizing.

On the other hand... He had been touched when he'd walked into the bedroom and seen her with Angelina. And later, when Emma had taken the little girl's thumb out of her mouth and kissed it, he had felt an overwhelming sense of gratitude because she had been kind to his child.

Wanting to make things right with Emma, and to have her understand the way it was, he said, "My wife died when Angelina was born. I tried for over a year to keep the children with me. I hired a whole series of housekeepers and nursemaids, but it didn't work out. I was at my wit's end when Mother stepped in and offered to take them. I know she can be difficult, but I also know that she does the best she can. They're better off with her than they would be with a stranger."

"Yes, perhaps they are." As anxious as he was to make up, Emma said, "I had no right saying what I did, Miguel. I hope you'll forgive me."

"There's nothing to forgive." He squeezed her hand, relieved that things were right between them once again.

* * *

Dainzu was a small but interesting site, with remains from several different periods between 300 B.C. and A.D. 1000. Miguel paid the small entrance fee, then led Emma to a pyramidlike structure. As they had been that stormy afternoon at Monte Alban, they were alone.

When he showed her the engravings along the steps of the pyramid, she began to photograph them. Again, as she had at both Monte Alban and Mitla, she used black-and-white film for a more dramatic effect.

When she had finished photographing the engravings, Miguel led her down some steps that led to a tomb.

"This dates back almost two thousand years," he told her. "Some experts believe the figures and tombs that have been uncovered are from the Olmecs, which might mean that the inhabitants of the Central Valley were related to them."

The tomb here, unlike the one at Monte Alban, had very few carvings. It was hot and dusty below, and although she was interested, Emma was relieved when Miguel led her back into the sunlight.

"Want to climb the pyramid?" he asked. "It isn't very high, but you'll have a better view of the site, as well as of the surrounding countryside, from the top."

When she agreed, Miguel took her arm and they started up the narrow and crumbling steps. When they reached the top, Emma took more photographs, then shaded her eyes with her hand and studied the deserted ruins below. "What were they like, do you think?" she mused aloud. "The people who lived here? And where did they go?"

"No one really knows for sure," Miguel replied. "Here in this area, as in the Yucatán, the people simply seemed to have vanished. Perhaps they were stricken by a plague. Perhaps, for whatever reason, they moved on to another place. It's a mystery that archaeologists and historians have been trying to solve for a long time."

"I came looking for facts and all I find is the mystery of a lost people," Emma said. "That bothers me, Miguel. I really want to know what happened to them. Do you think it was because of the Spanish? That because of them the people in this part of Mexico disappeared into the jungle, or maybe moved farther down into Central America?"

Miguel shook his head. "Most of them had already disappeared by the time the Spanish arrived."

"Then where did they go?"

He put an arm around her shoulders. "That's the mystery," he said with a smile. Then in a more serious voice went on to say, "Every time we make a new excavation or uncover a tomb, we hope to find an answer. Perhaps we will in the new tomb we've found at Monte Alban."

Emma turned to face him. "You thought I was prowling around, trying to find it, didn't you? That day we met at Monte Alban."

"Yes. Well . . ." He shrugged. "Maybe for a moment or two I did. You see, there had been prowlers that one of the guards routed only a few days before. It was long after closing time, no one else was around—"

"And I looked like a shady character," Emma finished.

"Exactly." Miguel grinned. "I could tell the minute I looked at you how dangerous you were." He reached for her hand. "Come on, let's start down. There's lots more I want to show you."

She'd never been good at climbing down from high places. Once, when she was six or seven, she had climbed into the hayloft of her grandmother's farm. Climbing up had been fun, but once there she'd looked down and decided that there was no way in the world she could climb down. The older cousin who had come with her coaxed and threatened. Nothing helped. Finally he had gone to get her grandmother and her mother. They had pleaded, threatened, promised a wonderful treat, anything, if only she would climb back down the ladder. She had shaken her head and retreated farther into the loft, until at last, driven by hunger and the plateful of brownies her grandmother had hurriedly baked, she had inched her way back down the ladder.

That's the way she felt about the narrow, crumbling steps of this pyramid, but she did all right until the third from the last step. Miguel, who had reached the bottom, still held her hand when suddenly she stumbled and skidded down onto one knee.

"*¡Cuidado!* Careful!" He helped her up. "Are you all right?"

"I think so."

"You've cut your knee."

"It's only a scrape."

He put his arm around her waist. "Come on over to the shade under the trees and let me have a look at it. You should have worn jeans today instead of a dress."

"I know. But I wanted to look more ladylike when I met your mother."

He squeezed her hand, and when they reached the trees and she sat down, he knelt beside her and with a clean handkerchief wiped the dust and dirt from her knee. When she winced he said, "Sorry."

"No, I'm the one who's sorry for being such a klutz."

"A klutz? I don't know that word."

"It means clumsy."

"You're not clumsy." He patted her leg. "There, that will do until we get to a pharmacy. Would you like to leave?"

"Not yet." Emma shook her head and lay back on the grass. It was a perfect day. Small white puffs of cloud drifted by. The sky was a cerulean blue and there was enough of a breeze to cool the air.

Miguel leaned against the trunk of the tree. "Tell me about your parents," he said. "What's your mother like?"

"My mother is every child's version of a fairy godmother. She's whimsical and enchanting and she writes wonderful stories of adventures in fairy-tale lands." Emma smiled as she looked up at him. "I honestly think she believes everything she writes, Miguel. That she really believes in places where anything is possible."

Emma stretched her arms above her head, looking up at the shadowed leaves of the giant tree. "She and my father are very different. He's a realist like I am. We both love my mother, but I'm not sure either of us understands her." She sighed. "When I was a child I wanted to be just like her. She's so small and pretty and delicate, everything I've always wanted to be.''

"I think who you are is just right." Miguel shoved away from the tree and came to lie beside her. "You have your own special beauty."

"I'm too tall."

"You're just right."

"I've always wanted to be short and cute."

"Cute is fine," he said. "But you're beautiful."

"No one has ever told me that."

"It's time someone did." He brushed a dark strand of hair off her face, and then he gently kissed her.

For a moment Emma didn't respond, she only lay there, arms resting against the grass, her lips quiet under his. Then slowly, like a blossom opening in the heat of the sun, her mouth softened and her lips parted.

She loved the warmth of his arms around her, and turned with him so they were lying side by side, their bodies close. He kissed her throat and whispered soft endearments in Spanish.

"Miguel," she murmured, so lost in his kisses she was not aware that he had cupped her breast until he rubbed his thumb across the waiting nipple.

His mouth was hot against hers and she was lost in his kisses, thrilled by the hand on her breast. When he opened the top buttons of her dress, she knew she should stop him, but didn't. He slipped the straps of her bra down, and then his hand covered her bare skin and he said, "Oh, yes." And kissed her breasts.

She whispered her pleasure and tightened her hands on his shoulders. "We shouldn't," she managed to say.

"I know," he said, but didn't stop.

"Someone might see us."

"There's no one here." He began to caress her, and when a sigh quivered through her and her arms tightened around him, he buried his face between her breasts. The softness of her, the scent and the feel of her inflamed him. He touched his tongue to one peaked nipple and was consumed with desire. He wanted her as he had never wanted a woman before. He wanted to take her here on the ground, in this strange and ancient place.

"We shouldn't..." she said again. But even as she protested, she lifted her body to his, as needy, as hungry as he.

He put both hands against the small of her back to bring her closer, and when he felt her heat through the thinness of her summer dress, the flame turned to a fire so bright it threatened to consume him.

Then she, too, was caught up in the wonderful frightening things that were happening. She felt his hardness against her and went weak with the knowledge of how much he wanted her. Flames tickled their way down to that most intimate part of her, and a longing unlike anything she had ever known possessed her. She wanted to get lost in him, wanted him. Wanted...

"Miguel," she whispered, and tried with weak and ineffectual hands to push him away.

"*Mi querida* Emma...Emma." He flicked his tongue across her breast.

She cried out and began to move against him, because she wanted this as much as he did. He cupped her bottom, bringing her closer. His mouth sought hers and they kissed with all the pent-up longing both of them were feeling, kissed and touched and moved together until with a muffled sob, Emma said, "No, we can't. We mustn't." And with an anguished cry she pulled away.

His breath came hard with the effort not to force her back into his arms.

"Please," she whispered.

He let her go and eased his throbbing body away from hers.

She lay there, her eyes closed, her chest rising and falling with each breath. For a moment Miguel didn't speak, then he said, in a voice that shook with all that he was feeling, "I'm sorry. I shouldn't have let it go that far. I didn't mean to."

"I know." She opened her eyes, and for a moment when she looked at him it was all he could do not to gather her in his arms again. Her mouth was tremulous, her lips swollen from his kisses. The sun, shining through the leaves, left dappled patterns of light on her bare breasts.

He bent and gently kissed her there. Then he rebuttoned her dress and, taking her hand, raised her to a sitting position. "This was my fault," he said.

She touched his lips. "No. I should have stopped you. It's supposed to be up to the woman."

He tried to smile. "It is?"

"I read someplace that it is."

He kissed her. Then he rolled to his feet and said, "Do you want to take more pictures?"

Emma shook her head. "I don't think I'm up to it. Because of my knee, I mean."

"I know what you mean. I'm sorry I forgot about your knee. I should have been more careful. Did I hurt you?"

"No." She brushed herself off, and when he stretched a hand down to her, she stood.

"We'll start back then." He picked up her camera and the camera bag, and together they walked to the car.

But all the way back to the city, Miguel was painfully aware of Emma beside him, and of the need that tightened his body. But in spite of that need there was a part of him that was relieved she had stopped it. She was different from the other women he had known, women he'd had casual relationships with, women he had left. Emma wasn't like those others. He didn't think that when and if they made love he would be able to casually walk away.

That gave him pause.

When they reached Oaxaca he dropped her off at her apartment.

He didn't want to let her go, didn't want her to turn and walk away from him. He was tempted to ask her not to. Tempted to say, "Let me come with you. Let us lie in your bed. Let me strip away your clothes and come into you. Let me..."

Instead he said, "Dinner at seven?"

"Yes, dinner." And when she touched his face, it seemed to him he saw a hint of disappointment in her eyes.

They walked from her apartment to a quiet restaurant on a quiet street. The lights were low, the food good. A lone guitarist strummed love songs.

They sat side by side at the candlelighted table. He gave her small bites of his steak, small sips of his wine. No one had ever done that before. Her father would have been horrified; her mother would have smiled.

He asked the guitarist to sing a certain love song, and when Emma did not understand the words, he softly sang them to her in English.

"You are as beautiful as the first flowers of spring,
Your skin in the shadowed moonlight is as delicate as the lily, as fragrant as the rose.
Open your arms to me. Come let me shelter you in the quiet of the night.
Come, my beloved, come to me."

He kissed her fingertips, her palm. She felt the hot moistness of his breath, and again, as it had under the trees, a flame warmed her body.

We need to talk about this, she wanted to tell him. It's going too fast for me. But the night was soft, the music was romantic and so was Miguel. Later, when she was alone, she would think about today, but for now, for tonight, she was content to be with him.

After dinner they strolled the few blocks to the *zocalo* and, like other lovers, walked arm in arm around the lovely old plaza. And sat on an iron bench and listened to the band play the old-fashioned Mexican ranch songs, songs of love and unrequited passion.

When at last Miguel took her back to her apartment, he made no attempt to come in. Instead he unlocked the door, and as he had that other night, handed her the key.

"We need to talk, *querida,*" he said. "But now is not the time. I have to fly to Mexico City tomorrow. I'll be gone for a week. We'll see each other when I return, yes?"

"Yes, Miguel."

He kissed her, and tried not to think of what it would be like to make love with her.

"Good night, my dear," he whispered. Then he turned and hurried out to his car.

She watched him go, and when he raised a hand in farewell, she waved, standing there in the doorway until he drove away.

Chapter 6

Miguel spent his days at the Museum of Anthropology and his nights thinking about Emma. Though he missed her, he needed this time away from her to sort out his feelings. Certainly at thirty-two he'd had his share of women, women who, like himself, were not interested in a permanent relationship.

He still knew two or three of the women he'd had affairs with, and after two almost sleepless nights, decided it was time to see one of them again.

He called Alicia Moro the following morning, and she squealed with delight when she heard his voice.

"Yes," she said. Of course she would have dinner with him.

"I'm in Mexico City for a week," he told her.

"Darling!" she exclaimed. "How wonderful."

He picked Alicia up at eight. She wore a low-cut black dress and three-inch heels. Her black hair curled becomingly about her piquantly beautiful face. She kissed him and, linking his arm through hers, leaned her slender body against him.

He knew halfway through dinner it wasn't any good; he didn't want to be with Alicia, he wanted to be with Emma. Over dessert he said, "I'm afraid I have bad news. I had a call late this afternoon. I have to go back to Oaxaca tomorrow."

Alicia's lips came together in a pout. "But, darling, I thought we'd have a whole week. I was looking forward to being with you."

"As I was with you," he lied, wondering how he could cut the evening short.

Alicia leaned across the table and he caught a glimpse of full, tanned breasts. "At least we have tonight," she said.

"I'm afraid not." Miguel looked at his watch. "I have some work to finish before I leave tomorrow."

"But, darling—"

"I'm sorry. We'll get together next time."

But he knew when he said it that there would be no next time.

He took her home. He kissed her cheek and felt like a heel because he knew she didn't understand. Nor did he. By the time he returned to his hotel, he was calling himself every kind of a fool. Alicia was a lovely woman and she'd been only too willing to resume their relationship.

Suddenly he was as angry at Emma Pilgrim as he was at himself. Angry because he didn't want to spend four or five nights with Alicia. And because all he could think about was Emma and the way he had felt when he'd kissed her.

Maybe I'll feel differently when I see her again, he told himself. And maybe, just maybe, the next time he wouldn't back away. He would make love to her, and hopefully that would get her out of his system

He left the following day on the noon plane for Oaxaca.

The pink roses were delivered late in the afternoon with a card that read, May I see you this evening?

Emma closed her eyes and breathed in the scent of the roses. She ran her lips across the soft petals and wondered why her hands were shaking. Miguel had been gone four days; it seemed longer. She had missed him more than she had thought she would. She could hardly wait to see him.

Because he hadn't mentioned what time he would arrive, or if they would have dinner, she wasn't sure how to dress. Finally she decided on a simple but elegant white blouse and a calf-length skirt, an outfit that, while casual, was still dressy.

He came at eight-thirty. He wore dark pants and an open-at-the-throat white shirt. His hair was still damp from his shower. He said, "I'm sorry it's late. I had some work I had to finish. I'd have called if you had a phone."

"It's all right." Emma held the door open for him. "Come in. Would you like a drink?"

"No, *gracias.*"

"How was your trip?"

"All right."

"You didn't stay as long as you planned."

"No." He took a step toward her, then stopped. "You haven't had dinner?"

"No."

"Neither have I. We'll get something."

She picked up her purse. He held the door open for her. He could smell her perfume and the clean fresh scent of her hair. He put his hand on her arm. "I've missed you," he said.

She looked up at him. "Me, too. Missed you, I mean."

"We'd better go."

"Yes."

But neither of them moved.

He touched her hair. "Emma," he said, and kissed her.

It was as he remembered. Her mouth was sweetly hot against his. Her lips were parted, tremulous. God, he thought, having her in my arms again is like coming home.

He let her go and stepped back. "Dinner first," he said.

She slipped her hand into his. "Yes, first," she answered.

They went to the same quiet restaurant on the same quiet street. Again, while the guitarist sang songs of love, Miguel held her hand. He kissed her fingertips and her palm, and once he gripped her leg beneath the table, kneading her thigh because he wanted so badly to touch her.

He wasn't sure what was happening to him or why this woman affected him the way she did. She looked very pretty tonight in her ladylike blouse and skirt, but it was more than that, more than the quiet elegance of her looks, the smoothness of her skin or the way her hair brushed her cheek when she leaned forward to tell him something. It was the essence of her, an unexplainable something that attracted him as no other woman ever had.

He wanted to say, "Let's forget dinner." Wanted to take her to some quiet place where they could be alone, to hold and be held by her, and do with her all of the things he had ever dreamed of doing with a woman.

Emma barely touched her food. Excitement built, but so did her uncertainty. She had thought a lot about Miguel these past few days, and she'd known as soon as she had seen him tonight that whatever it was between them, needed to be faced. She longed to be alone with him, but when he asked, "Are you ready to leave?" she felt a moment of panic. Would he want to go back to her apartment? And if he did, if they went in and closed the door behind them, what would happen?

But when they got into his car, he headed out of town instead of toward her apartment.

"I want to have a look around Monte Alban," he said. "Do you mind?"

"No, of course not."

"There's been a problem with one of the guards. I'd like to make sure he's on duty." He took her hand. "You're not tired?"

"No, I'm not tired."

"It won't take long."

"It's all right."

There were no lights on the hill that led to the historic site, but the moon was full, and with the beam of the headlights, he could see the road well enough.

When he pulled into the empty parking lot, he took a flashlight out of the glove compartment.

"Come with me," he said to Emma, and after he had opened her door, he took her hand and walked up the incline with her toward the ruins.

It was very quiet. There was no sound, not even of a night bird. Nor was there any sign of the guard who was supposed to have been on duty.

Miguel swore under his breath. This was what he'd been afraid of, why he had checked. Tomorrow he would hire another guard. No, two guards would be better, in case one of *them* didn't show up.

"Listen," Emma whispered beside him.

He tensed. "What is it?"

"The silence. Only the silence."

He felt it then, the magic and the mystery that existed here. He took her hand, glad that he was sharing this with her, and together they walked toward the deserted plain. The moon shone down, setting off in ghostly shadows the crumbling walls of the ancient city.

"It's as though they were only sleeping," Emma murmured. "All of the people who lived here before. As though they were still here—the children curled up together on straw mats or in hammocks. The husbands and wives . . ." She hesitated.

"Making love quietly in curtained-off rooms," Miguel finished.

"Yes," she said.

He touched her face with great tenderness because he knew that he was beginning to care for her, and because she felt about this place as he did.

Before them the pyramid rose, starkly beautiful in the moonlit night. And suddenly he wanted to be at the top of it, up where he could see the city spread before him. "Will you climb it with me?" he asked.

"If you'll hold my hand."

He took her hand and they began the climb up toward the top, where she had first seen him. Higher and higher they went, with the moon lighting their way. Emma was unafraid because he was with her.

When they reached the top, he led her toward the center of the platform and put his arm around her waist. In the distance they could see the lights of Oaxaca. And below, the three-thousand-year-old city that had been and was no more.

Miguel tightened his hand around Emma's, and when she looked up at him, he saw that her eyes were shining with tears. "What is it, my dear?"

In a voice so low he could barely hear, she said, "It's so beautiful. So somehow unbelievable." A sigh shuddered through her. "I'm glad you brought me here, Miguel. I'll never forget this night."

He thought then, as he had when he had seen the photographs she'd taken, how strange it was that this young *gringa* understood what all of this meant to him. She understood his love of this place, the strange and haunting mysticism of a lost civilization, of an ancient people who had disappeared forever.

He put his arms around her. He brought her close and held her, and together they stood looking out at the lost city below. They heard the faint whisper of the wind through the cottonwood trees, and saw against the moon the flight of a nighthawk and his mate.

She raised her gaze to follow the flight of the birds, and when she did, Miguel kissed her with all the pent-up longing he'd felt since that day at Dainzu. He kissed her and held her so close he could feel the beating of her heart.

"I've wanted this," he said against her lips. "Wanted you. Missed you."

Her arms came up to hold him as he held her, and she answered his kiss with a passion and a need that matched his own.

He cupped her face between his hands. He looked into her eyes. "Emma," he said. "Emma."

They kissed gently, then the kiss deepened and grew fierce with need. Their bodies pressed to each other, hungering, yearning. He pulled her blouse out of her skirt and put his hands under it so that he could touch her breasts.

"Emma," he whispered. "*Mi querida* Emma." He took her blouse off, and her bra. He looked at her there in the moonlight and knew as he bent to kiss her breasts that tonight he would not stop, that before the night was over he and Emma would be joined in love.

"I want you so much," he said against the coolness of her skin. "So very much."

She touched the side of his face. "As I want you," she whispered.

He brought her back into his arms and they held each other without speaking. "I want to feel your skin," she said. And when he took his shirt off she touched him with her hands and with her lips, and moving closer, rubbed her breasts against the hardness of his chest.

He moaned low in his throat. Gripping her shoulders, he held her away from him. Moonlight shadowed the fullness of her breasts with silvered softness.

"Look at you," he murmured. "*Por Dios,* Emma."

He kissed her again, and cupped her breasts, caressing, teasing, rubbing the roughness of his thumbs over the peaked and waiting nipples. And rejoiced when her body began to tremble and small incoherent cries issued from her lips.

He let her go long enough to yank at his shoes, then his trousers. He placed them down next to his shirt, and when he stood again and saw that she was watching him, he hooked his thumbs under his briefs and pulled them over his hips.

She looked at him, naked in the moonlight, and felt as though she could not breathe. He was magnificent, as splendid in his masculinity as the God of Renewal she had seen in the ancient tomb below. "Miguel," she whispered, and touched him.

A shudder ran through his body and she said, "Yes. Oh, yes."

He brought her into his arms and kissed her, so eager to take her that his body began to shake with need. He knelt on the stone platform, bringing her with him. He laid her on top of his shirt. He took her shoes off, then the skirt. He slipped her satin panties down over her hips and covered her naked body with his own.

"This is why I came back," he said against her lips. "Because of you, Emma. Because I knew we had to be like this."

He kissed her long and deeply, then, gripping her hips, he joined his body to hers.

She cried out, cried into the silence of the night with the sheer joy of having him inside her, and lifted her body to his, giving, receiving, rejoicing in the wonder of it. When he sought her mouth and whispered of his frantic need, she tightened her arms around his shoulders. "Miguel," she said. "Miguel."

His breath came in agonized gasps and she heard her own whimpered cries of a pleasure almost too great to bear as she came closer and closer to that final moment. When it arrived she cried aloud into the darkness of the night, and spiraled up and up into the moonlit night. He took her mouth, and with a cry his body convulsed with a terrible force over hers.

They held each other, heart beating against heart, breaths coming fast, but kissing, kissing as their arms tightened around each other.

"I've wanted this from that day at Dainzu," he said. "It's all I've thought about, the way it would be between us." He raised himself on his elbows and looked down at her. Her face was touched by moonlight, her eyes luminous. He kissed the lips that were swollen from his kisses. "We should have been in a bed," he said. "Not here on stone. I could have hurt you. I must have hurt you."

She smoothed a lock of hair off his face. "No," she said. "This was the right place, Miguel. This is where it should have been."

Here where I first saw you coming down out of the clouds. Here in this sacred place where others before us have loved.

He cradled her in his arms. He rubbed her back and gently kissed her. His body felt cleansed, surfeited. He was glad he had waited for this perfect moment with

Emma. It had been so unutterably right with her, so much more than it had ever been with anyone before. In a little while they would leave, but he would always remember how it had been, this night with Emma in this special place.

"Emma," he murmured into the stillness, and held her close to his beating heart while the nighthawk and its mate flew high above, and the wind whispered through the cottonwood trees.

They went back to her apartment. They undressed each other and showered together. Then he took the blue chenille spread off her bed and they lay down together.

He had not slept all night with a woman in a very long time, but he would sleep this night with Emma. He would hold her, caress her, and soothe her to sleep. But first...

He drew her into his arms and gently kissed her. "Again?" he said against her lips.

"Oh, yes."

Her arms crept up around his neck. He moved closer. She felt the strength of his arousal against her thigh, and the slow, sure climb to passion began.

"The light." She reached toward the nightstand.

But he stayed her hand. "No, I want to look at you." He folded the sheet back. "I want to see you and touch you." He ran a thumb across her lips. "It was too fast the first time. I hadn't meant it to be, but I couldn't wait because I'd thought about it for so long." He shook his head. "I want to make love to you properly this time." His fingers stroked her breasts. "I want to make us wait, Emma." He kissed her lips. "My Emma," he said.

He touched every inch of her with exquisite tenderness. He kissed her breasts until she whispered, "No more. Oh, please. Miguel, please. I want, I want..."

"I know." He rested his head against her breasts, and for a moment it seemed incredible to him that what he had dreamed of had come to pass. Emma was here with him, naked with him, his to touch and to caress. His to make deep and powerful love to.

He kissed her belly. He feathered kisses over her hips and stroked her legs. He cupped her in that special place with a touch as gentle as a feather brushing against her flesh.

And when he knew she could no longer bear it, he came up over her, to ease himself into her, to whisper his pleasure when she took him in. For this was Emma, Emma who wanted him as much as he wanted her.

He went slowly this time, taking her with him stroke for stroke, making her wait as he waited, moving deep within her velvet warmth. And when it became too much, when the excitement grew and he could not hold himself back, he tightened his arms around her, holding her close as he moved deeply, powerfully against her.

She lifted herself to him, crying small incoherent cries, murmuring his name, caught up in a whirlwind of emotion that rendered her helpless in his arms.

"Yes?" he cried. "Yes?"

But she was beyond words. She could only cling to Miguel as her body lifted to his, shattered by an ecstasy of feeling. Then, aware of his release, she took his cry and held him as he held her.

"Miguel, oh, Miguel," she whispered against his lips. And knew that after this night with him she would never be the same again.

They slept curled against each other. And woke to love again—slow, deep, lazy love.

Muted cries of passion in the darkness of the night. Whispered words...

"Was it good for you?"

"Oh, yes. Oh, yes."

He brought her head to rest against his shoulder. And wondered again what it was about her that made him feel a depth of emotion he had never felt before. She was a *gringa,* different from anyone he'd ever known. She had answered his passion with her passion. She had sought his mouth with eagerness and hunger. She had touched him unashamedly, and shivered with anticipation when he pulsated in her hand.

She was as different from Yolanda as night was from day.

He tried to push the thought of his dead wife away. It was unworthy of him to compare her to Emma. But he could not help himself. He and Yolanda had made love in that first burst of youthful passion, but from the moment she had thought she was pregnant, that had changed. She'd suffered him with stoic patience, and after she had become pregnant with Angelina, he had stopped all attempts at lovemaking.

Emma moved closer and kissed his shoulder. "I'm sleepy," she murmured.

"Then sleep, *querida.*"

"Don't leave."

"I won't."

She sighed, then her breathing evened and he knew she slept.

He stood at the top of the pyramid, naked except for the jaguar pelt that girded his loins. Tall and lean, skin bronzed in the setting sun, his expression serious, he looked down sternly at the people gathered below.

"It is the time of renewal," he said. "A time to begin again. A time of sacrifice...."

The crowd below grew silent, waiting.

"I have need of a maiden." His arm rose. He pointed. "You," he said, and with a gesture motioned for her to mount the stairs.

She came forward, trembling, her throat dry with fear of the unknown.

His eyes were dark, his cheekbones high and sharp. His mouth was sensuously cruel.

"Come," he said.

Step after step. Higher and higher she climbed. This was her duty; she did it for her people. It was her sacrifice to them. To him.

This priest. This warrior. This god.

He reached for her hand, and when she gave it to him he gripped it. "You tremble," he said.

She tried to speak but could not.

He led her toward the stone altar. When she tried to hold back, his grip tightened and he said, "The gods must be appeased."

He raised her up onto the sacrificial stone. He looked down at her, his eyes hooded with mystery. He removed the loincloth and stood naked before her.

"I have chosen well." His dark-as-the-night eyes burned into hers with an intensity that stopped the breath in her throat. He came to kneel beside her.

She felt the stone hard against her back, the sun on her face.

From below she heard the gasp of the crowd.

"Now you will belong to the gods," he said. He raised the deerskin dress and touched her in that most private of places.

She gasped.

He said, *"Querida?"* and began to stroke her there.

"You shouldn't."

He chuckled low in his throat. "Of course I should. So nice," he said. "So warm and nice, my sweet Emma."

"Miguel? I thought..." She opened her eyes. "I thought..."

"What, my dear?"

The dream, like cobwebs through the mist, began to fade. "The pyramid," she said. "I was a sacrifice for the god—"

"And worthy of a god." He kissed her. "But I'm only a man." He eased his body over hers, and they began the climb to perfect love.

In that final moment, when she lifted her body to his, it seemed to Emma that she could feel the coolness of stone beneath her back and the sun hot on her face.

Chapter 7

A week had passed since that night at the pyramid in Monte Alban, and during that week they had been together almost every day, and night.

They went to the archaeological sites of Lambityeco and Yugal. Emma took dozens of photographs and listened, fascinated, to Miguel's explanations of all he knew about the people who had lived there. Lambityeco, he told her, had probably been occupied from as early as 500 B.C. It was thought that the people there had moved to Yugal because it was a more defensible site in the time of trouble after Monte Alban had been abandoned. And Yugal, occupied by the Zapotecs, with Mixtec domination and influence, lasted until just before the Spanish conquest.

"So much is conjecture," he said when they stood in the Patio of the Triple Tomb at Yugal. "And information gleaned from what scientists have been able to transcribe from the glyphs and the geometric stone patterns.'' He pointed out the carved figure of a jaguar, and as he explained to her the jaguar's part in the history of his people, Emma remembered the dream she'd had of the man-god of Monte Alban.

She had thought often of the dream these past few days, and it seemed to her that sometimes, in the throes of making love with Miguel, that the man she had dreamed of merged with Miguel. It's a figment of your imagination, she told herself when that happened. But there were times when Miguel raised himself above her, when he gazed down at her with eyes hooded with passion, that it was not he but the God of Renewal who joined his body to hers.

She told herself it was because so many things had happened so quickly. She was in Mexico for the first time in her life—not in cosmopolitan Mexico City or Guadalajara, but here in southern Mexico, where things were more primitive. She was learning not only about Mexican culture, but of another, more ancient culture. She had met a man who was a descendant of that culture, a man who affected her as no other ever had.

She had always thought of herself as a realist, yet there had been times in the past few weeks when she had been besieged by fanciful ideas. On the night she and Miguel had made love atop the pyramid at Monte Alban, it had seemed to her that all of the people who had been there before were still there, that they were only sleeping. In the morning they would awaken and the city would once again begin to hum with activity. Children would play in the grassy square below, the women would grind corn and the smell of hot tortillas would permeate the air. The sweetmeat sellers and the feather merchants would ply their trades. The holy men would call to the gods of the sun and the rain to bring nourishment to their fields.

For the first time in her life Emma was allowing her imagination free rein and opening up to new thoughts and ideas. It was because of Miguel, because in a way she could not explain he had freed feelings she had not even known she was capable of.

She had a new awareness of her own sexuality, of feelings so intense, so overwhelming, they almost frightened her. Miguel had only to look at her in a certain way and her body would go weak with longing. Twice this past week they had left a restaurant, their dinner all but untouched, so anxious to be alone they could think of nothing else.

It was a kind of madness, Emma told herself, a madness she did not try to analyze or make sense of. She only knew how she felt when she was with Miguel.

She told him things she had never told anyone before, about Andrew Dillard, the boy in high school she had gone steady with, and how he had dumped her a week before graduation. And how it had felt to be the only girl in her class who hadn't gone to the prom.

She told him that when she was a child her mother had tried to dress her up in frilly dresses and hair bows, and how as soon as she rounded the corner of her street she had always yanked the hated bow off.

She told him how hard she had worked to become a really good photographer, and how important it was for her to succeed in her field. She shared hopes and dreams with him, all the time wondering why she felt compelled to do so.

He in turn talked about his children. "I feel a terrible sense of guilt because I don't spend as much time with them as I should," he confided. "I've let my mother take over the raising of them. I shouldn't have."

"They love you," Emma said.

"And I love them." A look of concern crossed his face. "Perhaps I don't show it. Perhaps I don't tell them as often as I should."

"Perhaps not," she said gently. "They're nice children, Miguel."

"Maybe in spite of me."

She stroked his face. "Because of you."

"You were very nice that day with Angelina."

"She's a sweet little girl." Emma hesitated. She wanted to tell him how much his small daughter needed his love, how much both children needed him. But she had overstepped once before; she didn't want to do it again. "You promised to take the children on a picnic," she said.

"I will," he said.

"When?"

He laughed. "You're an interesting woman, Señorita Pilgrim."

She smiled back at him. "What about this weekend?" she asked.

The next day Miguel telephoned his mother to say that he and Emma would like to take the children on a picnic. Saturday morning at ten they arrived at the house in Dos Santos. The children were waiting for them, Jose Antonio in clean white pants and shirt, Angelina in a starched pink dress.

Maria Leticia offered them coffee. Miguel said, *"Gracias,* Mother, but I think we'd better get started. We're going to stop at Santa Maria del Tule on the way. Neither Emma nor the children have ever seen it."

Maria Leticia turned to Emma. "The tree is more than two thousand years old," she said. "Like the archaeological sites, it is a part of our history. We are an ancient and a proud people, with a centuries-old culture unlike yours in the United States."

Emma forced a smile. "Mexico is a wonderful and an exciting place," she said. "But each country has its own special history, doesn't it?"

"Not as old as ours." Maria Leticia looked at the children. "Do what your father says," she told them. "Behave yourselves and don't get your clothes dirty."

She leaned down and Jose Antonio dutifully kissed her cheek. She ruffled his hair, then patted Angelina's shoulder. "Be a good girl," she said. "Mind your manners and obey your father."

Angelina took her thumb out of her mouth long enough to say, *"Sí, Abuela."*

Miguel kissed his mother's cheek and, hand in hand with his children, led the way out to the car. The children got into the back seat. Angelina arranged the skirt of her pink dress carefully. When they waved to their grandmother as they drove out of the yard, Maria Leticia called, "Be back early. The children go to bed at seven."

For a little while no one spoke, then into the silence Miguel said, "Señorita Pilgrim packed us a nice lunch.

If I'm not mistaken we have fried chicken and potato salad.''

"And chocolate brownies," Emma said in careful Spanish.

Jose Antonio grinned, but Angelina only looked at Emma, thumb in her mouth, her large dark eyes serious.

"Tell me about the tree at Tule," Emma said to Miguel. "Is it as big as they say?"

"It's a monster. Forty-two meters around. It's supposed to be the biggest tree in the world."

"It *is*," Jose Antonio said. "Grandmother said so."

"Then it must be true." Without conscious thought Miguel tightened his grip on the steering wheel. He loved his mother. Certainly he couldn't have managed without her these last few years. But there were times, like this morning, when he wanted to throttle her. She had been rude to Emma. He hadn't liked that, nor did he like what was happening to his children, especially to Angelina. The little girl was shy and withdrawn, and she rarely spoke above a whisper. He did not know what he was going to do about his mother, or how he was going to handle her. But something had to be done.

They passed through a small town and Emma said, "Can you stop?" She pointed to a general store. "I'd like to go in."

"Is there something we forgot?"

"Play clothes," she said.

"Play clothes?"

"For the children."

His dark eyebrows drew together, but before he could say anything Emma went on. "We're both wearing jeans—why can't they?"

Still frowning, Miguel stopped in front of the store. Emma turned and looked at Jose Antonio and Angelina. "Jose, you go with your father," she told him. "Angelina can come with me." She got out of the car, opened their door and, reaching for Angelina's hand, said in as good a Spanish as she could, "We're going to buy you something to play in. All right?"

The three-year-old, thumb in her mouth, looked doubtfully up at Emma. *"Mi abuela—"* she started to say.

"Will be pleased that you didn't get your pretty dress dirty."

And with an airy wave to Miguel and Jose Antonio, Emma led Angelina into the store. There she asked for the little girl's department and headed toward it, the still-silent child clinging to her hand. They found a pair of jeans that would fit, and when Angelina pointed to a bright red T-shirt with a blue parrot on the front, Emma said, "We'll take that, too."

For a moment Angelina was so pleased she forgot to suck her thumb.

Ten minutes later, with the starched pink dress in a box under her arm, Emma came out of the store, a transformed Angelina at her side. Miguel and Jose were leaning against the car. The boy was wearing jeans, a T-shirt and the widest grin Emma had ever seen.

Miguel was grinning, too. He hadn't liked Emma's being so high-handed about wanting his children to wear play clothes, but now, because he knew she had been right, he reached for her hand and squeezed it.

"That was a terrific idea," he said. "Thank you for suggesting it."

"Now we're ready for the picnic," she said.

They went to El Tule and Emma admitted that it certainly was the biggest tree she had ever seen. Jose Antonio ran around it twice, but Angelina, still shy, clung to her father's hand.

When they left they drove until they found a place that Miguel remembered having seen on the other side of Mitla, a flower-filled meadow with a stream that ran past big shady trees. He spread the blanket, then the red-and-white-checked tablecloth Emma had brought along, while Emma unpacked the picnic lunch.

"You see I was right," he said to the children. "We do have fried chicken."

"And potato salad and potato chips and lemonade." She set out the plates and knives and forks she'd brought from the apartment. Then the glasses and the big thermos of lemonade. "Would you like to play for a little while before we eat?" she asked.

Jose Antonio looked longingly at the stream.

"Maybe you would like to go..." She didn't know the word for wading, but she motioned toward the stream.

Jose looked from her to his father.

"It's all right if you'd like to, Joselito," Miguel said. "The lunch will keep."

The little boy sat down on the grass and pulled his shoes and socks off. Then, with his jeans rolled up to his knees, he ran toward the stream.

"Wouldn't you like to go with him, Angelina?" Emma asked.

The little girl shook her head.

"Then why don't we see if we can find some..." Emma looked at Miguel. "How do you say wildflowers?" she asked.

"Silvestres," he answered with a smile. "The two of you go ahead, I'll keep an eye on Jose."

Emma took his daughter's hand, and he watched them move out from the trees toward the meadow, Emma with her dark hair tied back from her face in a ponytail, Angelina with her braids flapping over her thin shoulders. Unexpectedly, he felt the sting of tears behind his eyelids, because he knew that he had neglected his children, that he hadn't been there for them the way he should have. It had taken Emma to show him that.

As he watched, Emma and his daughter began to run through the wild daisies. He heard a sudden squeal of laughter from his daughter and, like a blow to his heart, knew that he had not heard her laugh for a very long time.

Biting his lip, trying to hold back all of the emotions that were churning to the surface, Miguel turned and went down toward the stream to Jose Antonio.

In a little while Emma and Angelina returned, both of them clutching handfuls of daisies. Angelina helped Emma put the daisies in an extra glass and set the glass in the middle of the red-and-white tablecloth.

Jose Antonio jabbered in Spanish too fast for Emma to understand while he ate two chicken legs, a big helping of salad and almost a whole bag of potato chips. Angelina took only small helpings, but ate everything that was put on her plate.

"Limonada, por favor," she said. And Miguel poured her a glassful. She took a sip, but when she set it down, the glass tipped. Before her father could steady it, it spilled.

"Now see what you've done!" Jose cried.

The little chin began to wobble. *"Lo siento,* I'm sorry," she whispered. The big dark eyes filled with tears and she covered her face with her hands.

"Don't cry, sweetie." Emma pulled Angelina up onto her lap. "There's lots more lemonade."

"But she ruined the tablecloth," Jose Antonio said indignantly.

"We can move to the blanket." Emma smoothed the hair back off Angelina's face. "It's all right, *niña.* Truly it is." She put a finger under Angelina's chin and, lifting her face, kissed both cheeks and the turned-up nose. "We don't care about spilled lemonade. It's not important. You're important, Angelina. We care about you. This is your day, yours and Jose's. Your father and I just want the two of you to have a good time."

Miguel cleared his throat, then he poured more lemonade into her glass and said, "Don't cry, *querida.* Nobody's mad at you."

She sniffed.

"Have a potato chip," Jose said.

The suggestion of a smile curved Angelina's lips. She took the chip and slid off of Emma's lap. Miguel moved the food to the blanket and they went on with the picnic. And afterward, when they'd all helped Emma clean up, Angelina began tugging on her shoes.

"Go in the water," she announced.

"Is it all right?" Emma looked at Miguel, and when he nodded, she took Angelina's shoes and socks off and rolled up the child's jeans. "But you stay close to Jose Antonio," she said.

"No, you come."

"Okay." Emma shrugged, then took her shoes off and rolled up her own jeans. Catching each child by a hand, she said, "Last one in is a big green alligator."

They ran across the grass toward the stream, and as he watched them, Miguel heard again Angelina's little-girl laugh, and Jose saying, "I'm not an alligator, I'm a great big shark."

His children. He loved them, but it was difficult to express his love. He admired, more than he could ever express, the way Emma was with them, the way he wished he could be. But he and Emma were very different people. Right now she was twenty-five going on nine. Jose splashed her and she splashed him back, laughing when he looked astounded.

He didn't remember ever having been young. His father had been too busy tending to his business to spend much time with him. His mother had been loving but strict. There had been no after-school games for him. He had come directly home to do his homework. If there was playtime it was only on weekends.

He had married at seventeen. While other boys his age were...what was the American expression? Hanging out? Yes, while they were hanging out and having fun, he was trying to support a wife. There had been no more strolls around the town plaza on Sunday evenings while he and his friends flirted with girls. No more soccer games or going into the city to see an occasional bullfight. He was a husband, a man with responsibilities.

He lay down on the blanket, his shoulders against a tree, and watched the three of them. Jose had continued wading, but Emma and Angelina were picking up stones at the shore. They look like mother and daughter, he thought. And quickly sucked in a lungful of air. It was dangerous to think that way. Emma was only here for a month or two, then she would go back to her own country. She didn't belong here. He must not allow himself to think that she ever could.

He closed his eyes and pretended to be asleep, and though he hadn't planned on it, that's exactly what happened. He woke when he felt droplets of water on his arm. He opened his eyes and saw Angelina standing beside him.

"Look what I have," she said, and placed a smooth round stone in his hand.

Her bare feet were muddy and there were smears of mud on her face. But her eyes were excited and she was smiling.

"It's beautiful, *niña*," he said. "It's just about the nicest stone I've ever seen." Then he put his arms around her. He kissed both her dirty cheeks and hugged her close. "You're my girl," he said. "I love you, sweetheart. You do know that, don't you?"

She looked shyly up at him. Thumb in her mouth, she nodded.

He took the thumb away, and as Emma had done, he kissed it.

"Why can't Jose and I live with you?" She ducked her head, as though ashamed she had asked the question.

"Because..." Miguel hesitated. "It's because I work all day," he said. "And sometimes at night, too. There wouldn't be anybody to take care of you and Jose. That wouldn't be very good, would it?" He drew her closer. "When you're both in school it will be different. Then maybe we can all live together."

"How come I don't have a mother?"

"Because your mother is in heaven, sweetheart. But you have your grandmother and she loves you very much."

"Uh huh," she said. Then, "When we live together, can Emma come and live with us?"

That stopped him. "I don't think so, Angelina," he said carefully. "Emma lives in a different country, with her mother and father."

"But she's all grown up. Why couldn't she live with us?"

He didn't know what to say, so he changed the subject. "Don't you usually take a nap about this time?"

"Uh huh."

"Why don't you take one now?"

"I'm not sleepy."

"Maybe if you close your eyes you will be."

"Can I sleep on your lap?"

"Of course." He kissed the top of her head. "Go to sleep, baby," he said.

In a little while Emma returned. She put a pile of stones on the blanket and said, "Angelina saved the best one for you. She wants to take these home with her."

"My mother will love that." He smiled. "You're very good with the children," he said.

She looked at the sleeping child in his arms. "So are you."

"Am I?" Miguel shook his head. "I spend so little time with them, Emma. I'm not a very good father."

"You could be." She looked out to where Jose was still playing in the stream, and said, "I know your mother does the best she can, Miguel, but isn't there any way you could keep the children with you?"

He shook his head. "I tried to, Emma, but it just didn't work. Maybe when they're older and in school I'll try again."

You're missing so much, she wanted to say. You're missing all of their best years. But because she knew it would only make him angry or unhappy or both, she didn't say the words she wanted to. Instead she lay down on the blanket near him, and in a little while, like Angelina, she, too, went to sleep.

They stopped on the way back to Dos Santos to have dinner. The children had hamburgers and french fries, he and Emma had steak, and they all had cherry pie with vanilla ice cream for dessert.

It had been a wonderful day. Emma liked the children and enjoyed being with them. But now that the day was almost over, she wasn't looking forward to seeing Miguel's mother again, especially since it was long past seven.

Maria Leticia was waiting for them when they pulled up to the house a few minutes after eight. Arms crossed over her chest, she greeted them by saying, "It's late. Why didn't you call?"

Miguel got out of the car. "We stopped for dinner," he said. "There wasn't a telephone in the restaurant."

"The children should have been in bed an hour ago."

"One night won't hurt them." He helped Emma out of the car as Jose Antonio and Angelina scrambled out. Angelina took Emma's hand. "Come in the house with *Papá*," she said.

Maria Leticia drew her eyebrows together in a frown. "It's past your bedtime," she told Angelina. "Your father and Miss Pilgrim have to get back to the city. They—" Suddenly she became aware of what the children were wearing. "Why are you dressed that way?" she asked, sounding outraged. "Where are your clothes?"

"In a box." Jose reached into the back seat and took it out. "Emma said we should have different clothes to play in."

Maria Leticia's mouth tightened.

"I want *Papá* to put me to bed," Angelina said.

"You're not a baby," her grandmother started to say. "You can—"

"I'll take her in." Miguel picked the little girl up. "Say good-night to Emma, sweetheart."

She leaned out from Miguel's arms and kissed Emma's cheek. *"Buenas noches,"* she said.

"Buenas noches, sweetie," Emma answered.

"You, too, Jose Antonio. Tell Emma good-night."

The little boy shook hands with her. "Good night, Señorita Emma. Thank you for..." He screwed his face up, struggling for the word. "For the peek-neek," he said at last.

"You're welcome, Jose. We'll do it again soon. ¿Sí?"

"*Sí,*" he said and grinned at her.

"I'll only be a minute," Miguel said to Emma. "You go along with Mother."

She went inside. Jose Antonio disappeared down the hall after his father and Angelina, and she was left standing in the living room with his mother.

"Would you care for a cup of coffee?" Maria Leticia asked, and headed for the kitchen.

"No, thank you." Emma opened her purse and took out the plastic bag of pebbles Angelina had picked up and handed it to the other woman. "These are the stones that Angelina found today," she said.

"Stones? What nonsense." And with that Maria Leticia opened the garbage pail and threw them in. "Angelina won't remember," she said, "and I certainly don't want them littering the house."

"But..." Emma bit back her objections. In a careful voice she said, "Small things are important to children. Maybe if you let her keep them for a day or two—"

"Do you have children, Señorita Pilgrim?"

"No, *señora.*"

"Then what makes you an authority?" Her nostrils pinched with anger, Maria Leticia glared at Emma. "I suggest you leave the raising of my son's children to me," she said. "And I also suggest that my son is far too busy to act as a tour guide—"

"Mother!" Miguel stepped into the kitchen. His eyes, so like his mother's, were angry. He put a protective arm around Emma. "My mother is tired," he said to Emma. "She didn't mean to be rude." He looked at his mother. "Did you?" he asked.

For a moment Maria Leticia didn't answer. Her mouth twitched. "No," she said at last. "*Lo siento.* I'm sorry. I was worried because the children were late."

Emma nodded, but said nothing.

"We'll be going now." Miguel guided Emma out of the room. "I told the children I'd pick them up next Saturday morning. We're going to spend the weekend at the *choza.*"

His mother looked from him to Emma, one dark eyebrow raised in a question she did not ask. "What time would you like them to be ready?"

"About nine, if that's not too early."

Maria Leticia nodded.

"And let them wear the clothes we got for them today."

"Very well."

He went to his mother, kissed her cheek. "*Buenas noches, Madre,*" he said. "Until next weekend."

"Good night, Miguel." She nodded to Emma. "Miss Pilgrim."

"Good night, *señora.*"

Maria Leticia went out to the car with them. She said a stiff, "*Buenas noches,*" then turned and marched back into the house.

"I'm sorry," Emma said, not sure what it was she was apologizing for.

Miguel leaned over and kissed her. "No, *querida,* I am the one who is sorry. You will have to excuse my mother. I've never brought a woman to her house before. For some reason it upsets her that I brought you."

Emma rested her head back against the seat. Because I'm a *gringa?* she wondered. Or because she thinks there might be something serious between us?

Was it serious? Was Miguel beginning to care about her as much as she...? She stopped in midthought, not sure it was something she wanted to think about. Not yet.

He pulled her closer and she leaned her head against his shoulder.

"It was a wonderful day," she said. She liked his children and she...liked him? She looked up at him and he kissed her. And she knew that what she felt was so much more than like.

Chapter 8

It was a little before nine on Saturday morning when Miguel pulled into his mother's driveway. Before he could open his door, both children bounded down the front steps calling, *"Hola, Papá. Hola,* Señorita Emma."

"Hola, Joselito. *Hola,* Angelina." Miguel hugged both of them and said, "Are you ready for the weekend?"

They nodded excitedly, then ran toward Emma when she got out of the car. She, too, hugged them, and when she let them go, said *"Buenos dias,"* to Miguel's mother. "It's a nice day for an outing, isn't it?"

"Sí." Maria Leticia's mouth was pinched. She handed a small suitcase to Miguel. "May I see you inside?" she asked.

"Of course." He put the suitcase in the car and to the children said, "Wait here with Emma. I'll only be a minute."

"Is something wrong?" he asked once he and his mother were inside.

"Of course something is wrong!" She faced him, her dark eyes blazing with anger. "You're going to spend the weekend with that—that woman! With your children there! How dare you do such a thing? How dare you?"

"There are two bedrooms in the *choza*," Miguel said as calmly as he could. "Emma will sleep in one of them with Angelina, and I'll be in the other with Jose Antonio."

Arms crossed over her chest, her expression serious and accusing, Maria Leticia said, "I have seen the two of you together, you with your arms around her. I have seen you kissing her in the car. That's disgraceful conduct, especially in front of the children."

"It doesn't hurt them to see affection between a man and a woman," Miguel cut in angrily. "God knows I saw little enough of it when I was growing up."

He had said the words before he'd thought. But they were true; he had rarely seen any display of affection between his mother and father. Every evening when his father came home from his shop, the dinner had been on the table and the house spotless. But in all of his growing-up years Miguel had never seen his mother greet his father with a kiss or an affectionate look.

"I'm thirty-two years old, Mother," he said quietly. "What I do with my life is my business. I'm fond of Emma and I see no harm in showing my affection for her in front of the children. I see no reason why Emma and I shouldn't be together for as long as she's here.''

''How long will that be?''

''Another few weeks. I'm not sure.''

''Then this...whatever it is between you will be finished?''

Finished? The word struck him with a terrible finality. He had told himself before that night at Monte Alban that once he made love to Emma he would be able to put all thoughts of her behind him. But the reverse had happened. Each time they made love it only whetted his appetite for more. He would leave her in the morning, sated after a night of lovemaking, and two hours later find himself thinking about her, and of how it had been with them only a few hours before. His body would tighten and it would be all he could do not to get in his car and drive like a wild man to her apartment. It was as though now, in his thirties, he was experiencing all the intense sexual feelings that young men in their late teens and twenties usually felt.

Yet he had been able to say to his mother, in a calm and reasonable voice, that Emma would leave in a few weeks. Would it be finished when Emma left? He had no answer, because he could not yet face the fact of Emma's going away.

So he said, ''I don't know. But it's my affair and I'll handle it.'' He looked at his watch and, eager to end their conversation, said, ''We'd really better get going.''

''When will you be back?''

"Early Monday morning." Miguel rested his hand on her shoulder. "I should take the children more often than I do, to give you a break. I know they're a handful and I hope you know how much I appreciate the care you give them."

"I only do my Christian duty," his mother said.

Miguel looked at her. He wanted to tell her that he didn't want her to do it because it was her Christian duty, he wanted her to do it because she loved Jose Antonio and Angelina. Because he was her son, because she loved him.

He hesitated, then, knowing he couldn't change her, he kissed her cheek, and with an *"Adiós,"* hurried out to the car.

Emma had thought that a *choza* would be something like a summer place, with all of the amenities that made for easy weekend living. Miguel had told her when they'd first met that a *choza* was a rustic cabin, but she was sure his idea of rustic was the same as her idea of a cottage.

But when they turned off the road onto what was little more than a cow path, she began to wonder.

"Now you can see why I brought the pickup," Miguel said with a grin.

The cow path wound up into the hills, past farmers leading their cows to greener pastures, past a boy taking a pig down the road to market. And once, on the curve of a hill, Miguel slowed to pass an old woman leading three burros. A baby burro, no bigger than an average-size dog, followed behind.

"Ohh!" Angelina, who was sitting on Emma's lap, leaned out of the window. "Look at the baby," she said, and Miguel stopped the car so that she could see the small animal.

"Could I pet him?" she asked.

"I don't see why not." He said something to the woman, who nodded, and swatting her string of burros, urged them to the side of the path.

Angelina and Jose Antonio got out of the car. Jose scratched the burro's ears and Angelina patted his nose. Looking up at her father, the little girl asked, "Can we take him with us?"

"I'm afraid not, sweetheart. Tell the burro good-bye and thank the lady for letting us see him."

Her lower lip came out, but she said, *"Gracias, señora,"* and obediently climbed back into the pickup with Jose.

Now and then, as they rounded a curve, Emma caught sight of a small wooden house with a thatched palm roof leaning precariously on the side of a hill. And once she asked, "Do people really live in them?"

"Of course." Miguel grinned at her. "Those, *mi querida gringa,* are *chozas.*"

Her earlier vision of a picturesque summer cottage fled. Was Miguel's *choza* like the ones they passed? And if it was, how in the world would she last the weekend?

A few minutes later they left the cow path and started up a smaller, rutted path. "We're almost there," he said, and Emma braced herself for the worst.

Soon afterward he said, "There it is, through the trees."

It was a cabin with a thatched palm roof, bigger than the others they had passed, but still a cabin. With indoor plumbing? Emma wondered as she followed Miguel and the children out of the car.

Trees grew close to the cabin—white acacias, golden feather palms, fern palms and a blossoming royal poinciana. Crimson bougainvillea grew at random, as did yellow hibiscus and orange trumpet vines. Spider lilies were everywhere. There was a small vegetable garden at one side of the house, a field of hollyhocks beyond. It was all very beautiful and wild, and Emma wasn't sure how she felt about it.

Miguel picked up the suitcases. "I haven't been here in several weeks," he said as he opened the door and motioned Emma inside. "I sent a message to one of the neighbors to come in yesterday and clean. I hope it's not in too bad a shape."

It wasn't. Actually, Emma thought, it looked quite comfortable. There was a black leather sofa in the living room, along with two matching easy chairs, end tables, oil lamps and a desk. Bookcases lined one wall; two rifles hung on another.

"The kitchen is in here." Miguel, hefting bags of groceries, headed toward a curtained-off partition.

There was a table with four chairs, shelves filled with canned goods, other shelves holding plain white dishes. Pots and pans hung from hooks over the black wood stove.

A wood stove? She barely got by with a modern electric range and a microwave. What was she supposed to do with a wood stove?

"The facilities are out back."

That answered her question about indoor plumbing.

"I'll get ice from the village as soon as I put these things away." Miguel indicated the old-fashioned icebox. "A couple of blocks should be enough to last us through the weekend."

"Right." Emma cleared her throat and said, in what she hoped was a cheerful voice, "You go ahead, I'll take care of things here."

She reached for a can of tuna, but he stopped her. "What do you think of my *choza?*" he asked.

"It's...uh, very nice. The children seem to like it here."

"What about you?"

She looked around the small kitchen. "It's different," she said.

"Yes." He put the tuna fish on the shelf. Eyebrows drawn together in a frown, he started to say something else, then shook his head and said, "If you can manage, I'll run over to the village."

"Fine." Emma avoided his eyes and busied herself with the groceries, knowing full well she should have shown more enthusiasm. But she couldn't help being shocked. She hadn't expected to find a mansion in the hills, but neither had she expected to find anything this primitive. She was a city girl; this would take some getting used to.

When Jose Antonio called out that he was going to the village with his father, Angelina came into the kitchen with Emma. When the food they'd brought had been put away, Emma said, "Maybe we should unpack now. Your father said there were two bedrooms. Which one would you like?"

"The big one," the little girl said, and taking Emma's hand, led her into the room to the right of the living room.

There were curtains, but no screen on the window. A breath of wind rustled through the thatched ceiling-roof, and Emma had visions of wild creatures scooting around up top, and coming through the window at night.

There was a double bed, a dresser on which rested an oil lamp, a wardrobe and a chair. When Emma didn't see a closet, she said, "Where should we hang our clothes?"

"In there." Angelina pointed to the wardrobe and opened her suitcase. "This is *our* room," she said shyly. "Do you like it?"

"It's..." Emma searched for the right words, and at last said, *"Muy bonito."*

Angelina nodded, and taking Emma's hand, said, "Let's go outside and play."

That's where they were when Miguel and Jose Antonio returned. Miguel carried the two blocks of ice into the cabin and put them in the icebox. "I'll fix lunch," he said. And when Emma offered to help, he shook his head. "I'll do it," he said, and she knew he was upset with her.

They ate ham sandwiches at the kitchen table. The two children drank milk; Emma had a soft drink, Miguel a beer. Jose and Angelina did most of the talking, and as soon as they'd eaten, went outside to play.

When he and Emma were alone, Miguel said, "I'm sorry you don't like the place."

"I didn't say I didn't like it."

"Didn't you?" He looked at her intently. "There's something I want you to understand," he said. "This is part of who I am, Emma. My grandfather built this cabin. My father was born on a straw mat in the bedroom."

His dark eyes were intent on hers. "I'm an educated man," he said, "a modern man. I have an air-conditioned condo in the city and I drive an air-conditioned car. But that's only a part of who I am. This is the other part, the Indian part. You need to know that."

She nodded slowly, trying to understand. But it was difficult, because she had been raised in such a completely different culture. She had grown up with television and electric lights and a toilet that flushed. She was used to turning on a light switch, to having ice cubes in her drink, and a hot bath when she wanted one. Friends had invited her on a camping trip two years ago. She had gone, but she'd hated every minute of it. Now here she was in a rustic cabin with Miguel and his two children, and she honestly didn't know how she felt about that.

For supper Miguel cooked hamburgers on the wood stove while she prepared a salad. After they had eaten, they lighted the oil lamps and sat in the living room playing word games. When Angelina began to nod, Emma said, "I'll take her in to bed."

She picked the child up just as something rustled in the bushes outside the door. "What's that?" she asked, startled.

"A small animal," Miguel said. "Maybe an iguana. They're harmless."

She took Angelina's hand. At the door of the bedroom, she hesitated. "I'm a little tired," she said. "I think I'll go to bed, too."

Miguel's mouth tightened. "Very well," he said.

"We'll see you in the morning."

"Fine." Getting out of his chair, he picked Angelina up and kissed her. "*Buenas noches, niña,*" he said. "Sleep well." He looked at Emma. "You, too," he added. But he made no attempt to kiss her.

She and the little girl started into the dark room. "You have to light the lamp," Angelina said.

"Oh." Emma looked at Miguel. "We have to light the lamp," she said.

"I'll light it. Meantime maybe you'd better take Angelina outside."

"Outside?"

"To use the bathroom."

"Oh," she said.

He handed her a flashlight. "Angelina knows where it is."

With thoughts of the animal they'd heard rustling through the bushes, Emma took Angelina's hand. They made their way down a path in back of the house. The facilities were clean but primitive.

When they returned to the cabin, Miguel said, "The lamp is on, but you'd better turn it off as soon as you can so the mosquitoes don't come in."

The mosquitoes and what else? Emma thought again of the rustling they'd heard in the bushes earlier. "Good night," she said, and closed the door.

She undressed the little girl and put her nightgown on before she turned off the lamp and undressed herself.

"It's pretty dark, isn't it?" she said to Angelina.

"Just like at grandmother's. She says only silly people are afraid of the dark. I'm not afraid, at least not most of the time. I..." Something rustled in the bushes outside the window. "What's that?" Angelina sat straight up in bed.

"Probably just an iguana," Emma said, and hoped it was true. She got into bed and put an arm around the little girl.

"You won't go anywhere, will you?" Angelina asked in a trembling voice.

"No, baby. I'm going to be right here all night."

Angelina snuggled closer. "You're nice, Emma," she said, and closing her eyes, went almost immediately to sleep.

It was a strange feeling, holding a sleeping child in her arms. It was something Emma had never done before and it made her feel protective, as though she would do anything she had to to keep this child safe from harm. The little girl was so tiny, so unbelievably fragile, so dear. Emma kissed the top of Angelina's head. Miguel's child, she thought.

She had disappointed him today. She was sorry she had and promised herself she would make it up to him tomorrow. She would do her absolute damnedest to make him think she liked his *choza*.

One more day, one more night. She could pretend for that long, couldn't she?

On the way back from the facilities next morning Emma saw an iguana dart out onto the path in front of her. She screamed and ran back to the cabin.

"It was only an iguana." Jose Antonio shook his head and looked disgusted. "It wouldn't hurt you."

And when Miguel, with a smile, said, "I could ride shotgun the next time," she wasn't amused.

He pumped water from the well so that she could bathe Angelina, then showed her how to work the makeshift shower he had rigged up near the back door. While she bathed, he fixed breakfast. Afterward he suggested they all go for a walk, but Emma, remembering the iguana, declined. She knew she wasn't being a good sport, but she couldn't seem to help it. She wanted to be back in her own apartment, with electric lights and a bathroom.

When Miguel and the children returned from their walk, he said to Emma, "I know you're not having a very good time, so we've decided to leave tonight instead of in the morning."

"But I am," she said, trying to sound convincing. "I'm having a fine time."

For a moment Miguel didn't respond, then he shook his head and said, "It's best we leave tonight."

And so it was that after dinner they started the trip back to Dos Santos. When they reached Miguel's mother's house, Angelina and Jose Antonio told Emma goodbye. Angelina hugged her. "I wish you lived with Jose and me," she whispered. "But don't tell Grandmother."

"I won't." Emma tightened her arms around the small body. And felt a terrible sense of loss when she let Angelina go.

On the drive to the city, Miguel said, "I'm sorry you didn't enjoy the weekend. I shouldn't have asked you to come."

Emma wanted to tell him that he was wrong, that she'd had a great time and that she really loved his cabin, but she couldn't. All she could say was, "I'm sorry, Miguel. I guess I'm just not the outdoor type."

"What type are you, Emma?"

She didn't answer. She wanted to slink lower into the seat, to tell him how sorry she was that she had ruined his and the children's weekend.

I'll make it up to him tonight, she told herself. It will be all right when we're together again. I'll show him how much I care.

He pulled up in front of her apartment and parked. He took her to the door, and when he had opened it, said, "It's late. I'd better let you get some rest."

"But aren't you..." She swallowed hard. "Aren't you coming in?"

He shook his head. "I've got a lot to do tomorrow and I want to get an early start." He looked at her, then away. "I'm going back out to the cabin," he said. "I'll take some work along and do it there."

"How—how long do you think you'll stay?"

"Three or four days. Maybe a week." He handed her the key. "I'll see you when I get back."

"But..." She gripped the edge of the door. "Are you sure you don't want to come in?"

"It's late." He kissed her, a quick, unemotional kiss. "Good night, Emma," he said.

When he turned away, she closed the door and stood there, silent, stunned. She looked at the light he had snapped on when he opened the door. She heard the hum of the electric refrigerator. Modern conveniences.

She went into her bedroom and sat on the edge of the bed, and knew that she had never felt quite this alone before.

Miguel wasn't sure why it mattered so much to him that Emma hadn't liked the cabin. He didn't go there often, but he loved it when he did, and it had been important to him to take her there. But it had been a mistake; he'd known that as soon as they'd pulled up in front and he'd seen the expression on her face. She hadn't been comfortable. She hadn't liked anything about the cabin.

He had wanted her to know and understand this part of him. But she hadn't understood.

His father had brought him to the *choza* when he was very young. He had loved it, as he had loved his father's parents. They were warm and loving people, and he'd spent as much of his growing-up years with them as he could.

His grandfather, Nicasio, had farmed a large piece of land near their home, and whenever Miguel was there, usually during his summer vacation, he'd helped his grandfather. He wore the same clothes his grandfather wore—white cotton pants tied at the ankle, a white shirt, a wide-brimmed straw hat and huaraches.

"I want to be just like you when I grow up, *Abuelo*," he would say.

And his grandfather would answer, "You are already like me, my boy. But some day when you are older you will be more than a farmer. You will go to the city to get an education, and when you are a man you will be someone of importance, a man who will contribute knowledge and skill to our country.'' Nicasio had rested a hand on Miguel's shoulder. "But you must never forget that you are a part of all this, Miguelito. This land belongs to you, just as it belongs to me. It is a part of you, and some day when you are older you will discover that it is the best part.''

Miguel's grandmother had died when he was sixteen, his grandfather while he was in Mexico City going to the university. The old man had left the *choza* to Miguel.

During the first few years after his grandfather's death Miguel had had little time to go to the cabin. But recently he had found himself going there more and more. He had fixed the place up, added an extra room and bought new furniture to replace the old.

It was his refuge, the place to which he retreated when his life became too stressful. People spoke of returning to their roots. This was where his roots were, here in this simple *choza,* not in the bigger, the colder house in Dos Santos.

That's why he had wanted to bring Emma here. He had wanted to tell her about his grandfather. He had wanted her to understand what all of this meant to him.

But she hadn't understood. He needed to think about that.

Chapter 9

Emma slept little that night. The next day she tried to work on the article she had started on Mitla, but she couldn't concentrate. She'd write a sentence, then stop and stare out of the window. Finally she went into the darkroom to develop the roll of film she'd taken at Yugal. She worked automatically, without inspiration. The pictures were fine, okay, nothing special.

When she finished in the darkroom, she went for a walk. It was early afternoon and in the *zocalo* young lovers strolled arm in arm, looking at each other with love-struck eyes. She had a cup of coffee at an outside café, and returned to the apartment for a lonely dinner of scrambled eggs and toast.

Miguel would be at the *choza* now. The oil lamps would be lighted. The thatched roof would rustle in the wind, but except for that whispered rustle, everything would be silent. He'd be sitting in one of the black leather chairs, or perhaps, if the light was good, he would be at the desk, working on whatever it was he had brought with him. In a little while he would go to bed, alone. As would she.

It rained that night. She thought of the way the rain would sound on the thatched roof, and slept fitfully. When she awoke the rain had stopped, but the sky was gray and threatening. She looked out at the wet streets. And thought about Miguel.

As soon as the rain stopped, Miguel started out across the land where his grandfather had toiled so long ago. The fields lay fallow now, and as he walked along the rutted ground he thought about what it would be like to bring them to life. To plant corn or barley or wheat and see these fields come to life once again.

He could hire one of the farmers from the village to tend the land and he would come as often as he could to oversee things. He would teach Jose Antonio and Angelina all of the things his grandfather had taught him. And when he had other children . . .

But he would have no other children. He would never marry again.

He walked for a long time, and when the sky grew dark and thunder rolled across the sky, he headed back to the cabin.

The rain started a half hour after Emma left the city, in a car she had rented that afternoon. It had a stick shift, and all she'd ever driven were automatics. The rental agent said, when he turned it over to her, *"Muy fácil, señorita.* It is very easy. Yes? *Uno, dos, tres, quatro* and reverse. No problem. *¿Si?"*

But there was a problem, because every time Emma slowed the car for a stop sign or a turn, she forgot to shift. And when she did remember she forgot to use the clutch. She'd been jerking to a stop and stalling for almost an hour now, trying to see through the rain, certain she'd never find the cow path that led to the path that led to the cabin.

She had not made a conscious decision to come. She had gotten up, made a breakfast that she couldn't eat, and been on her second cup of coffee when she suddenly stood up and went into the bedroom. She packed two pairs of shorts, T-shirts, her toothbrush and hairbrush in an overnight bag, pulled on a pair of jeans and a clean white shirt and headed for the door. It occurred to her halfway there that she needed transportation, so she'd looked for a rental-car agency in the telephone book. They'd said they had a wonderful car that was in perfect condition. It turned out to be a 1979 model that was far from new.

It didn't matter. She was on her way to Miguel.

"Please let me find the road," she kept saying under her breath. "Please let him be there."

The rain became a full-blown storm. Thunder crashed and lightning split the sky. There were almost no other cars on the road and she slowed to a snail's pace, frantically searching for the turnoff. She would have missed it if a streak of lightning hadn't lit the sky just as she drove past. She stopped, grinding the gears as she searched for reverse, muttering and swearing under her breath until at last she found it and backed up the car.

The cow path hadn't been great before, but now it was almost impassable. She crawled along at five miles an hour, trying to see through rain-slashed, fogged-up windows, until at last she saw the rutted path off to the right.

"Thank God," Emma said, and turned into it. Just then the car coughed and died.

"Oh, damn," she muttered. "Hell and damnation!"

She turned the key. Nothing happened. She tried again and again, but the car wouldn't start.

She had two choices: she could sit there fuming and wait until the rain stopped, if it ever *did* stop, or she could walk.

"So I walk," she said aloud. Taking a deep breath, she opened her door and stepped out into the rain. Within seconds she was soaked.

As near as she could remember, they had driven five or ten minutes after the turnoff from the cow path until they reached the cabin. So that meant it was...what? Two miles? Three?

The path was awash with mud. It came up to her ankles; it lapped at her feet. Twice she lost her sling-backed sandals. And once she cried aloud, "What's a city girl like me doing in a place like this?"

But she kept going, because she had to see Miguel, had to tell him she was sorry. That it really didn't matter that his *choza* didn't have indoor plumbing or electric lights, she just wanted to be where he was.

She slogged along the muddy, rutted path. Once she tripped and fell facedown in the mud, and, slipping and sliding, fought her way to her feet again.

The clouds lowered. Soon it would be dark. That worried her. What if Miguel hadn't come to his cabin after all? What if he was back in Oaxaca and the cabin was locked? What if...? Then, through the darkness, she saw a light, and with a glad cry started toward it. The rain and the mud didn't matter now. She was almost there. Almost to Miguel.

He was in the kitchen heating a pot of coffee when he heard a noise that sounded like someone knocking. But that was impossible. No one in his right mind would be out in weather like this.

It sounded again and he headed for the door, muttering, "Who in the hell...?"

He opened the door. His eyes widened. Emma stood there dripping, covered with mud, her wet hair straggling over her eyes. He said, "Emma? Emma? What are you...?" He took her arm and pulled her inside. "How did you get here?"

"I rented a car." She started to shake, partly from the chill, partly from nerves. "It broke down," she said. "I had to walk."

He couldn't believe she was there. For a moment he could only stare at her, but when he realized she was wet and shaking with cold, he said, "Come in," and led her into the kitchen. "Get out of your wet clothes," he said. "I'll find you a towel and something for you to wear."

"I had a suitcase, but I left it in the car."

"We'll worry about that later," he called over his shoulder as he hurried out of the room.

He couldn't believe she was here; he had no idea why she'd come. He took one of his shirts out of a dresser drawer, his slippers from under the bed, and went back into the kitchen.

When he returned, she was standing at the sink pumping water, scrubbing at her face and arms, her bare back to him.

"I'm a mess," she said when she heard him. "I'm dripping mud all over the floor."

"It doesn't matter." He handed the towel to her, and when she had dried herself and cleaned her feet, she put on his shirt and slippers.

He poured her a cup of coffee, then one for himself, and said, "Let's go into the other room."

Emma followed him. The blue denim shirt covered her to midthigh; the too-big slippers slapped the floor with every step. She curled her legs under her on the black leather sofa and took the coffee. Sipping it gave her an excuse not to talk. She was embarrassed now and terribly nervous, not sure she should have come. Miguel had had little to say. Was he glad she'd come, or was he upset?

For a few moments they drank their coffee without speaking. "I hope it's all right," she said. "My coming here, I mean."

"Of course it's all right." He moved to sit at the other end of the sofa. "But I'm not sure why you did, Emma."

"Neither am I." She gave him a lopsided smile. "Well, maybe I am." She put her cup down on the table in front of her. "You were upset because I didn't like it here, because I felt uncomfortable. And it's true, Miguel. I did feel uncomfortable."

"Then why did you come back?"

"I had to see you, to make things right between us. Because if this is a part of who you are, I want to like it, too."

"Why?" he asked. "Why, Emma?"

She hesitated for a moment. "Because I care, Miguel. I care about you."

The words were simple, softly spoken and heartfelt.

He moved closer so that he could put his arms around her, and when he did he felt the tension in her body. "I was wrong to be angry," he said.

"No." She shook her head. "You wanted me to like it as much as you do, and when I didn't you were disappointed." She looked up at him. "Tell me why it means so much to you."

He settled back against the sofa and pulled her closer. "The *choza* belonged to my father's parents," he said. "I used to come here during the summer. There were only two rooms then. My grandparents slept in one of them. I slept on a *petate,* a straw mat, in the other."

"On a straw mat?" she asked in surprise.

Miguel nodded. "My mother couldn't understand why I wanted to be here, but I loved my grandparents, especially my grandfather. His name was Nicasio. He was as tall as I am now, but very thin and spare. He owned five acres of land, and every morning at sunrise he would set out on his mule to tend them. When I was here I would go with him. I don't know how much help I was, but I loved being with the old man. He told me stories of what the country around here had been like when he was a boy. And he told me of the ancients who had lived here thousands

of years before. I think that's when it started, Emma,
my interest in archaeology, I mean. There was so much
I wanted to know about those people, about how they
lived, what they ate, how they made clothes. Nicasio
wasn't an educated man, but he told me what little he
knew and said that when I grew up I should go to a
university and learn about those things."

Miguel shifted a little so that he could look at
Emma. "He was a wonderful man," he said. "He and
my grandmother, Rosa, were married for almost sixty
years. They loved each other and they loved me. I feel
closer to them when I'm here."

She touched his face. "I'm sorry I didn't understand," she said.

"No, it's all right. I shouldn't have expected you to.
You're from a different country, a different culture."
He smiled gently. "You're a *gringa*."

I can be anything you want me to be, Emma wanted
to say. I want to be *tu mujer,* your woman, Miguel.
But because she dared not say the words, she lifted her
face to his and kissed him. He tightened his arms
around her, and suddenly everything was all right
again. She felt safe and warm. Passion would come,
but for now it was enough to be held.

He kissed her. He whispered her name against her
lips, and opened the shirt that covered her nakedness.

The flame began. Deep inside her it grew and
spread, snaking down through her belly to the apex of
her legs, setting her afire, making her weak with
longing.

Miguel eased her back against the leather sofa, half
covering her body with his.

"Mi querida," he said against her throat. *"Mi linda mujer."* He pressed hot kisses over her shoulders and her breasts, and when her arms crept up to hold him, he knew a moment of perfect joy because she was in his arms again.

He cupped a breast, gently caressing it with his fingertips, coming closer and ever closer to the tip. And all the while he kissed her with hunger and passion, feeling her lips part and the sweet moistness of her tongue touching his. He heard her soft whisper of pleasure, and his body swelled with a desire he could barely hold in check.

Her skin was cool from the rain, and he ran his face back and forth across the fullness of her breasts, murmuring incoherent words of desire, taking first one, then the other rosy nipple in his mouth to gently suckle.

She moaned aloud, twisting her body under his, whispering, "Miguel, Miguel."

Oh, yes, he thought. Whisper my name like that, my Emma. Let me know you want me as I want you.

She tightened her hands in his hair and said, "Oh, please! Oh, darling, please!"

He circled a breast with his tongue, lapping, sucking, loving her frantic movements, her whispered pleas. He ran one hand down her belly, feeling the smoothness of her naked skin come alive to his touch. He cupped her and touched her. She took his mouth from her breasts and kissed him, her mouth hungry against his.

He answered her kiss, his mouth hot and moist against hers, feeling as though his body would explode, knowing that he had to take her quickly.

He sat up, yanked down his jeans and kicked them away. Then he was on top of her, feeling the whole silken length of her. She gripped his shoulders, he gripped her hips, and then he was inside her, moving hard against her while she lifted her body to his.

His body thundered against hers, hard and deep and hungry, and still she lifted herself to him, holding him, asking no quarter, giving none.

She licked his shoulder. She ran her hands down the length of his back, over the hard buttocks, then pressed both hands against the small of his back, urging him on, loving what he was doing to her, with her. She wanted this to go on and on, even as she reached toward the peak of that ultimate moment. *Wait!* she wanted to cry. *I don't want this to end.*

She tightened her arms around him, seeking his mouth, wanting to tell him how splendid this was. But she was incapable of words. He kissed her and her body rose to his in a dizzying explosion of feeling that made her cry out into the stillness of the room. Up and up she soared, close and clinging. And when it began for him she gripped his shoulders, saying, "Oh, darling. Darling."

His body shook with reaction. He held her close, gasping for air. What was happening to him? he wondered through the dizzying aftermath of passion. He had never felt so much. It was as though Emma had discovered a hidden depth within him that he had not known was there. She had shaken him to the very roots of his being, plumbing feelings he had not thought himself capable of. It went far beyond good sex, although God knew it had been that. When he had joined his body to hers he had become a part of her, and she a part of him. For the briefest fraction of an instant it was as though their souls had touched. In that moment he had somehow changed. He didn't know how or why, he only knew that it was so.

He moved slightly away from her and brought her head to rest upon his shoulder. He stroked her sweat-slick body and kissed her brow.

But he did not tell her all that was in his heart.

In a little while they got up. He pulled on his jeans; she wrapped his shirt around her. Barefoot, they padded out to the kitchen. He added wood to the stove and opened a can of soup. She found the crackers and put them on the table.

They smiled at each other over the flame of the oil lamp.

And when they had eaten, they went into the bedroom and lay side by side in bed.

"Thank you for coming back," Miguel said.

Emma raised herself up and kissed his chest. "I had to. I couldn't leave things that way between us."

"We can go back to the city tomorrow if you want to."

"No, I'd like to stay here."

"Even though we don't have indoor plumbing?"

She groaned and leaned her head against his shoulder. "Even though," she said.

Thunder rumbled in the distance and they heard the first drops of rain against the thatched roof. "It's a good sound," Emma said, and snuggled closer.

Miguel put his arms around her, hardly able to believe that she was here, that she had come back to him. Now that their passion had eased, it was wonderful to hold her this way, to know that when he awoke she would be here beside him. That tomorrow and for all the tomorrows they had left, they would be together.

He thought then of how it would be when she returned to the United States and knew that he did not want her to leave. What would she say, he wondered, if he were to ask her to stay? If he said, *Stay with me for a while?*

How long was awhile? Three months? Four? And after that?

He rubbed his chin against her hair. We're very different, he thought. She doesn't belong here, any more than I belong in her world.

He had traveled in the United States, in Central America and in Europe, but Mexico was his home. He loved his people and the work he did. He loved toiling day after day in the hot sun of southern Mexico, waiting and hoping for that breathless moment when a discovery was made, when he could hold in his hands some remnant of a past civilization.

He felt like that about the new tomb they had uncovered in Monte Alban. They had dug in only partway, but already he and his crew had brought out treasures from the past—gold and silver ornaments, turquoise necklaces, pieces of pottery, glyphs that would take months, even years to decipher.

His life was here, his profession, his children.... But what about Emma? he asked himself. What part does she play in my life? How can I let her go?

She rested her hand on his thigh. Then, half-asleep, she began to caress him.

It started again, that quick rise to passion. With a cry he turned to her, and when he said her name there was the sound of desperation in his voice.

He kissed her and told her in Spanish how she made him feel, then he raised her over his hips.

"Oh!" she said, surprised. Then, with a little sigh, she settled herself onto him.

They began to move together, rocking slowly, letting it build. He caressed her breasts. She moved her body against his, and in the shadowed darkness of the room he looked up at her. The soft dark hair splayed over her shoulders and her naked breasts. Her eyes were half closed, her delicate nostrils pinched with all that she was feeling.

For me, he thought. For me.

He tightened his hands on her hips and his body heaved hard under hers. With a cry she grasped his shoulders and he felt her body begin to quiver. He didn't want it to end and so he tried to hold her, to quiet her. But she was beyond holding back, just as he was. He fought for control, knew that he was losing it, that nothing could stop him now.

She was wild and wonderful above him and he let her go, urging her on, reaching now for her breasts, crying out in an agony of pleasure, "Yes! Now, yes! Love, oh love."

She collapsed over him, holding him as she sought his mouth. And her body shook with the reaction of all that she was feeling.

He held her. He stroked her shoulders and her back. He told her how fine she was and how she made him feel. He said love words in Spanish that she didn't understand.

And when she'd grown quiet he said, "Sleep this way, Emma. Over me. Cover me." And he tightened his arms around her so that she wouldn't leave him.

Leave him. He could not bear to think about that.

Chapter 10

The days that followed were the happiest Emma had ever known. She learned to cook on the wood stove and no longer shuddered when small creatures skittered out of the bushes. She almost got used to the outdoor facilities.

The morning after her arrival she and Miguel walked back to where she had left the car. "Battery's dead," he said. "They had no business giving you this piece of junk."

"The man there said it was all they had."

Miguel swore in Spanish. "They saw you coming, *querida*. I'll call them as soon as I get to the village and have them pick it up." He attached cables from his car, and when it started, he drove back to the cabin and let Emma follow in his car.

"Now I can wear my own clothes," she said when at last she opened her suitcase.

"But I like you just the way you are." He reached under the shirt and patted her bare bottom.

"And this is the way you'd like to keep me," Emma retorted with a smile. "Barefoot and..." She stopped.

"And what?" he asked.

Emma shook her head. "It's just an expression."

"Tell me."

"Barefoot and pregnant."

"Oh." Miguel looked uncomfortable. "We haven't discussed that, have we? Pregnancy, I mean. We should have."

"I'm on the pill. I started on it just before I came to Mexico. The doctor suggested I start before I left the country. I'm pretty sure everything is all right."

A look of relief crossed his face. "Thank God!" he said.

Emma wasn't sure why that hurt, but it did. Everything between them had happened so fast. She hadn't stopped to think or to reason, she had simply accepted the way she felt about Miguel as something special and wonderful.

She hadn't known until she'd come out to the cabin that this was the beginning of love.

She had never been in love before. She'd been in *like* a couple of times, but these feelings for Miguel were totally different. There was a whole mixture of emotions involved in the way she felt about him—happiness, excitement, uncertainty and bewilderment. She was more aware of everything around her. The sky was bluer, the grass greener. Flowers smelled better and food was tastier. She went to sleep every night to the music of crickets and cicadas, and awoke to the song of birds. She was more alive than she had been in years.

Miguel, too, seemed different at his *choza* in the hills. It was for him a time of getting back to the basics, to the way of life he had lived as a child here with his grandparents.

In the city he usually dressed in conservative business suits, or tailored pants and shirts. But here he wore the typical Indian dress of the area—white cotton pants tied at the ankle, full-sleeved white shirts and huaraches. They were the clothes Emma had first seen him in that day at the pyramid in Monte Alban, and though she liked the more sophisticated part of him, in a way she could not explain, this was the man she loved best.

There were times when she awoke in the night and would lay quite still, listening to Miguel's even breathing, feeling his warmth next to her. She would think about Nicasio and Rosa, and how they had lived and loved in this place for sixty years. What would it be like, she wondered, to live with a man that long? To lie with him night after night, to make love so many thousands of times?

And suddenly, lying there in the dark, Emma knew that she wanted to be like Nicasio's wife. She wanted to be married to Miguel, to love him, to be with him and to sleep by his side for as long as they lived.

He had never told her he loved her, nor had he ever said that he didn't want her to leave. But he would, she told herself. When the time comes for me to leave he won't let me go.

She listened to the sound of his breathing and she was overwhelmed with love, by the depth of feeling she had for this man. If he did not love her... No, she wouldn't think about that. For surely he could not be as he was with her if he didn't love her.

Every morning Miguel worked on the papers and books he had brought with him. Emma had left in such a hurry she hadn't thought about anything except getting to Miguel. Now, with the help of two of his archaeological books that were in English, she began work on an article that would fit in with the series she was writing.

In two days they developed a routine of sorts. They worked until noon, then stopped for lunch—quesadillas dripping with warm cheese and hot salsa, or a salad of sliced mango, papaya and pineapple. They talked about what they had been working on, and one such noon he showed her photographs of the glyphs that had been taken from the walls of the newly uncovered tomb, glyphs that he was painstakingly trying to interpret.

"They'll tell us a lot," he said. "When we finish deciphering them it will be like opening a new page of history."

"I wonder if it will tell where they went, the people who carved the glyphs." Emma rested her hand on his shoulder and looked down at the photographs. "Were these taken before I came?"

"Some of them." He clamped down on the sudden suspicion that arose at her interest. This was Emma and he trusted her. He saw the beginning of a frown and quickly said, "We have an official photographer, Emma. A man who has government clearance."

"Can I at least see the tomb?"

Miguel shook his head. "It will be awhile before it's open to the public. I'd take you in if I could, but it's dangerous right now with the excavations still going on. Maybe in a month or two—"

"I won't be here in a month or two," she said, disappointed. "I'm almost finished with the articles. When they're done..." She looked at Miguel, then away. "When they're done it will be time for me to go home."

He reached for her hand and pulled her onto his lap, and there was an expression in his eyes she had never seen before. "You're a writer," he said. "Writers can work anywhere."

"I have a house in Denver, Miguel. My life is there."

He tightened his arms around her. Don't leave me, he wanted to say. Stay here with me. Be here for me. But God help him, he wasn't sure he was ready for the kind of commitment Emma needed. He hadn't known her long, but long enough to know she wasn't a part-time woman. For Emma it would be all or nothing. He needed time to think about that.

He kissed her. "We don't have to talk about it now," he said, and tried not to see the sadness in her eyes. Instead he made himself joke and say, "Besides, when the time comes I may decide to keep you here, locked away in my *choza*."

Barefoot but not pregnant, Emma thought.

He picked her up and carried her to the sofa, and because of the sadness he had seen in her eyes, he began to make love to her with great tenderness. As he touched her he thought of all the things he liked about her—her warm and throaty laugh, her style and her elegance, her intelligence. The way she was with his children, and how she fit into the *choza* now that she had come back to him. She pressed closer and with a muffled cry began to stroke him in turn. And her passion, he thought. I love her passion.

With the realization that she might leave him, his arms tightened around her and suddenly the love-making changed. He wanted to possess her, to make her his so that she would never leave him. He became like those ancient men who had come before him, the warriors who had conquered, who had taken what they wanted—land and gold and women. As he was taking Emma.

He thrust his body hard against hers, and heard her small gasp of surprise. The sound of it, of the whisper of her voice in the silence of the room, inflamed him. He took her mouth, plunging his tongue against her as he plunged his manhood into her softness, that primitive part of him wanting to punish her because she had talked of leaving him.

Her arms crept up around his neck and she lifted her body to his. She said, "Miguel. Oh, Miguel."

And as suddenly as it had come, his anger vanished and he felt the hot sting of tears behind his eyelids. His movements slowed, his mouth softened on hers. He drew her into the shelter of his arms, and together, slowly, gently, they shared that final moment of ecstasy.

He was very quiet the rest of the day. He worked at his desk with a magnifying glass, going over the photographs, making notes, his brow wrinkled as he tried to concentrate. But at last, because he couldn't, he put the photographs aside and said, "Tell me about your life in Denver. Where do you live? Do you see your family often?"

"I have a small house in a new section of town," Emma answered. "I bought it a year ago because I needed space for a darkroom. My living room faces the mountains, and I have a backyard where I can sun in the summer."

"Nude?"

She laughed. "Of course not. The neighbors would be shocked."

"Do you see your parents often? Do you live far from them?"

"I'm about thirty minutes away. And yes, I see them at least once a week."

"In Mexico a young woman lives at home until she's married," he said.

"No matter how old she is?"

Miguel nodded. "If she's sixty-five and unmarried, she lives at home under the protection of her family."

"That's terrible!"

"It isn't terrible at all. Unmarried women belong with their parents."

"Good grief!" Emma glared at him. "I've lived alone since I got out of college when I was twenty-one."

He muttered something in Spanish she didn't understand. "You were too young," he said. "Too vulnerable. You still are."

"So I suppose I should live with my parents until I'm sixty-five?"

"Yes, if you don't marry."

But she would marry, and the thought of it—of Emma being married, of her ever being with another man as she was with him—was unthinkable. And because it made him angry, he said, "You're not Mexican, you don't understand."

"No, I don't." She was silent for a moment or two, then she reached for his hand. "We're very different," she said.

His anger faded as quickly as it had come, to be replaced by a gut-deep sadness. She was right; they were different. And he didn't think she would ever want to live his kind of a life. He knew he would never live hers.

On their last day at the *choza* they went to Monte Alban. "I need to check on the progress of the new tomb," Miguel said. "Next week I'll be working inside it. I want to see what's been going on."

"I can wander around and make a few more notes." Emma wished she had brought her cameras, but she hadn't. Which meant she'd have to make another trip to Monte Alban before she left Mexico. The thought of leaving saddened her and she said little on the trip to the archaeological site.

"You go ahead," she told Miguel when they arrived. "I'll wander around."

"Don't climb the pyramid," he cautioned.

"Only with you," she answered with a smile.

But Miguel did not smile. She would not go to the pyramid with anyone else, but someday, if he let her go, she would *be* with someone else. Caught in a blackening grip of desperation, he looked at her for a moment, then turned away.

The tomb smelled of dust and old bones. By the light of the lanterns strung there, Miguel saw that the work had not progressed as much as he had thought it would. One of the heavy stone slabs covered with hieroglyphs in the antechamber had been carefully swept clean. The other had not. Farther inside he inspected the frescoes that were similar to those of Teotihuacán in Mexico City.

The carved figure on the left of the inner chamber was the God of Renewal, the one on the right the God of Rain. Many of the funeral offerings had already been taken into the working part of the museum, where they would be dusted and studied, but he was sure there were more still to be discovered.

Now that he had seen the tomb again he was anxious to get back to work in it. Research and extensive reading were necessary, but if truth were told, he was happiest on his hands and knees digging into the past.

When he saw that almost two hours had gone by, he left the tomb and went into the museum to check on what had been done with the artifacts that had been taken there. When he finished he went out to find Emma.

She was sitting on the lower step of the ball court, looking up at the pyramid. She didn't see him, and he stood there for a few moments watching her. She was wearing jeans and a red-and-white-striped T-shirt, and she had on an old straw hat she had found at the cabin. Her face was pensive, and he wondered if she was thinking about the night they had made love there at the very top of the pyramid. For as long as he lived he would never forget how it had been that first time with Emma.

He started toward her, and when he called her name she turned and lifted her arm in a wave.

"Have you been waiting long?" he asked as he gave her his hand to help her up.

She shook her head. "I just sat down a few minutes ago. Are you ready to leave?"

He nodded. "It will be our last night at the *choza*. I thought we'd have a special dinner."

"Then you'd better cook it," Emma said with a laugh.

"I intend to."

She poked him in the ribs with her elbow. "I don't know how your grandmother managed all those years on that old wood stove. She had to have been a wonder."

"She was. She cooked and cleaned, did her laundry in a tin tub, kept a vegetable garden, and managed to have twelve children in her spare time."

"Twelve children! You're right, she was a wonder." Emma linked her arm through his. "What are we having for dinner?"

"*Carne asada* and a bottle of red wine."

"By lamplight. That's nice, Miguel." She looked at the package he was carrying. "More research?" she asked.

"Something like that."

They made the trip from Monte Alban in an hour, and it was almost dark by the time they reached the cabin.

"I'm hot and dusty," Emma said. "I'll bathe first, if that's all right with you?"

"Of course, go ahead."

She took her shower out behind the cabin. The water, though cool in the early morning, had been warmed by the sun during the day. She still wasn't used to the heat in Oaxaca, and the shower cooled and refreshed her. When she'd finished, she wrapped a towel around her body and went back into the kitchen.

"Better?" Miguel kissed her and held her away from him. "Come into the other room," he said. "I have a present for you. Two presents, actually."

"Presents?" Emma's eyes widened with excitement. "Where?"

"Here." He handed her the package he'd brought from Monte Alban. "I hope it fits," he said.

They went into the living room. She sat on the sofa and opened the package. "Oh," she said. "Oh, my," and pulled out a long, coarsely woven off-white dress. The front was embroidered in intricate designs, in colors of brown and gray, beige and off-white. It was simple, Indian in design, and, in its own fashion, quietly elegant.

Emma stood and held it up. "It's beautiful," she said softly. "Thank you, Miguel."

"It's the kind of a dress my grandmother wore on special occasions. I thought perhaps you'd like to wear it tonight."

"Of course." She took the towel off and pulled the white dress over her head. The sleeves were long and full and the rough fabric felt cool against her skin. "I love it, Miguel," she said, and kissed him. "Thank you. It's a beautiful present."

"This is for you, too." He handed her a smaller package, and when she opened it, she saw a large gold pendant that was perhaps five inches long and hung in a series of five linked pieces. The first was an intricately carved figure of the God of Renewal. A round disk with a star was next, then the God of Corn, a jaguar and a butterfly. From that were strung four bell-like cylinders. The whole thing hung on a heavy gold chain. It was the most spectacular piece of jewelry Emma had ever seen.

"It's magnificent," she said a little breathlessly.

"I bought it in the museum today. It's a replica of an original piece that dates back more than two thousand years." He slipped it over her head. "I hope you like it, Emma."

"Like it?" Her eyes filled. "It's beautiful, Miguel. I don't know how I can thank you."

"I do." He smiled and put his arms around her. "I'll think of a dozen ways before the night is through."

"And so will I." She lifted her face for his kiss. There were so many things she wanted to say, that she was afraid to say. And so she said only, "Thank you, darling," and kissed him.

They had dinner at a small table in the living room so that they could look out at the white acacia and the royal poinciana trees. When day faded into evening they lighted the lamps, and toasted each other with red wine and tender kisses.

Miguel had changed into a fresh pair of the white cotton, Indian-style pants and shirt he had worn all week. Emma had brushed her hair and fashioned it into a thick braid. Her face was devoid of makeup, and with the Indian dress and the replica of the two-thousand-year-old necklace, she could have been a woman from the past.

It came to him as he looked at her that this is what it might have been like for his grandparents when they were younger. That on just such a night as this they, too, had eaten their supper here in the pale glow of the oil lamp. And afterward they would have made love, as he and Emma would soon make love.

Nothing really changes, Miguel thought. Love is the same whether it be on a straw mat in a cabin like this or on a canopied bed in the finest hotel. If two people care about each other, the where or the when don't matter, all that really matters is the loving.

Yet he did not know if he was ready for that kind of love or for the kind of commitment loving Emma would mean.

Loving Emma. It was a sobering thought.

The rain began just as they were preparing for bed. "I hope it won't last," Miguel said, thinking of how impassable the path to the main road became in the rain. "If it does we'll be stuck here for another day or two."

"Is that so bad?" Emma sighed, and reached for his hand. "This has been such a happy week, Miguel. I'll never forget this time we've spent together at your *choza.*

He pulled her into his arms. "Nor will I," he whispered against her hair.

He wanted to tell her then that he did not want her to leave him, but there were so many things to consider. His children; he had to think about them. They were his responsibility and he knew that he had not really accepted that responsibility as he should have. He would remedy that. He would be a better father than he had been because Emma had helped him to see how much Jose Antonio and Angelina needed him.

And, too, he had to consider all the cultural differences between himself and Emma. He had been shocked when she'd told him she had lived alone since she was twenty-one. And she had been shocked at what she considered his old-fashioned ideas. But that was what he believed, the way he would shelter Angelina until she married. The way it would be with any other daughters he might have.

And as Emma lay silent beside him, Miguel thought of what it would be like to have a daughter with her, a little girl who would look just like her. He would be protective of their daughter, and when she grew older he would want to kill the young men who flocked around her. His and Emma's daughter. The product of their love.

He heard the rain against the thatched roof, a soft rain that would stop before morning. He sighed and drew Emma closer. He kissed her and caressed her, and knew that tonight would be a night of love.

His mouth was gentle as it whispered upon her skin. He scattered kisses over her face, her throat, over her shoulders to her breasts. He kissed her breasts for a long time, savoring the rounded softness, the peaked, rosebud nipples. He feathered kisses down her belly and her thighs. He kissed her in that most special of places, and held her there as her excitement grew, held her until her body writhed and she cried out, and whispered his name over and over into the silence of the night.

And when at last he eased his body over hers, he said, "Again for me, my Emma. Again, *mi amor, mi vida, mi preciosa.*"

He moved against her in a frenzy of desire, merging his body with hers, making her a part of him, but holding himself back, making himself wait until it began again for her. Only when she lifted her body to his did he allow his cadence to quicken. Only then did he give full rein to his passion, his overwhelming passion for Emma.

He heard that sweet and final cry, and gripped her with his arms and with his legs, his body strong and powerful against hers, on fire with need as he drove hard toward that final moment. And when it came he cried a great and primitive cry.

Now it was she who stroked his back, who soothed him with loving words and gentle touches while he lay spent in her arms.

"The rain has stopped," she said after a little while. "Look, Miguel, you can see the moon."

It shone in through the window, a faint stream of silver light. He raised himself up on one elbow so that he could look at Emma. Her hair was tousled about her face. He saw the faint sheen of sweat on her naked body, naked except for the heavy gold pendant that hung between her breasts.

He touched it. It was not cold as it had been when he'd bought it today, but warm now from her body. "I wonder who she was," he mused, "the woman who wore the original piece."

"Someone very special to have received such a gift."

"As you are special." He kissed the tips of her breasts, then turned so that she lay close in his arms.

They slept and in a little while awoke to love again. This time he brought Emma up over him. With a sleepy sigh she settled herself upon him. Hands clasping his shoulders, she began to move against him.

"Yes," he said. "Like that, yes."

He looked up and saw her body silvered by the moonlight. And the gold necklace that hung down, like a remembrance of the past, between her breasts.

He closed his eyes and as he surged against her she became the woman from the past. He gave himself up to her, to Emma who had become her, and in his mind's eye he saw them, the man and woman as they might have been those hundreds of years before.

He opened his eyes and looked up at Emma. His woman then, he thought. But my woman now.

Chapter 11

Miguel spent the next few days at the tomb in Monte Alban. It was hot and dirty work, but he loved every minute of the time he spent there, for he was discovering the past, delving into ancient secrets of the proud people who had lived and died so very long ago. While Europe was still in the Dark Ages, more than twenty-five thousand people had inhabited Monte Alban. Like the Maya and the Aztecs, they had built cities and roadways, a system of irrigation. They had traded with other cities farther to the north, and they had built temples and pyramids, the remnants of which still existed today. As did their tombs.

This was the work that Miguel loved; this was the place he would never leave.

While he worked in the tomb, Emma was busy on the series of articles she had been commissioned to write. She was doing the editing now, and pleased with what she had produced.

"But I need to take a few more photographs at Monte Alban," she told Miguel over dinner three days after they had returned from the cabin.

"Then come out in the morning with me," he said. "When you're finished you can take a bus or a taxi back to the city."

He spent the night with her, and at seven the next morning they drove out to Monte Alban together.

"I'm going to work for a couple of hours in the tomb before I go to the museum," he said. "I brought new artifacts out yesterday and I want to spend some time cleaning them today." He kissed her and told her to take it easy. "It's going to be hot," he said. "Try to finish by noon."

"I will," she promised, and watched him walk away toward the tomb. The new excavation fascinated her, and she would have given anything to see it. Even one photograph along with the others she had taken at Monte Alban would add an additional sense of mystery to the articles she was writing. What harm would one photo do? By the time her articles came out the archaeological world would already know about the discovery of the tomb.

All the while she took pictures of the Gran Plaza, the ball court and the south platform, she thought about the tomb and how much she wanted to photograph it.

By eleven-thirty she'd taken several rolls of film, all of the photographs she needed. Miguel had said he was going to be in the tomb only for a couple of hours. By now he'd very likely be in the museum. She started back the way she had come that morning. The guard who had seen her with Miguel earlier waved. She waved back, then went around the corner of the palacio, out of sight.

The tomb lay ten yards away, half-hidden behind a stand of pepper trees. There was no one around. One picture of the entrance, she thought. I won't go any farther than that.

But when she had taken her picture, she couldn't resist stepping inside the tomb. The noonday sun slanted in, casting shadows. The air was dry and cool, the atmosphere eerie and mysterious. It smelled dry, as the dust of bones it enclosed.

The walls were covered with geometric designs, with deer and jaguar figures stained in red and turquoise green. Though the designs had faded over the centuries, they were still remarkably clear. Farther into the tomb she saw heavy stone slabs covered with hieroglyphs, and she began to photograph them. Then she got down on her knees to photograph close-up the remnants of pottery, of bowls and urns and statues, that had yet to be taken out of the earth and cleaned.

It was wonderful, better than she had even dared to hope. These were the photographs that would make her articles strong and riveting.

She stood, about to leave, and saw before her a carved figure of the God of Renewal. As he had the first time she had seen him in the other tomb, he took her breath away. Never had she seen such strength of form, such overwhelming masculinity. She hadn't taken a picture of him the first time, but she would now. She focused and snapped, once, twice, three times for good measure, then stepped away.

The god stared at her with his stone eyes and for a moment she couldn't move. Then, tentatively, almost fearfully, she reached out to touch his face. The stone warmed beneath her fingertips and she stood as though mesmerized, scarcely daring to breathe.

Don't leave, those stone eyes seemed to say. Stay with me. Be with me. Do not leave me.

"But I must," she whispered, filled with a sudden sadness she could not explain.

She went out into the sunlight and stood in the shade of the pepper trees, feeling unsteady, almost giddy. From the sun, she told herself. Because I came too quickly from darkness into the light. And she told herself she had to leave before anyone saw her there, before Miguel returned.

She would tell him what she had done, of course, and though he might be angry, he would forgive her when he saw the photographs.

A bus arrived just as she descended the stairs to the parking lot and she rode back to the city, so eager to develop the photographs she'd taken that she could hardly wait to get into her darkroom.

When at last she did, she lost herself in her work. The photos of the glyphs and the stained walls were even better than she had hoped. So were the pictures of the pottery. They expressed better than any written words the mystery of the tomb that had been sealed off for the last three thousand years. You could almost smell the dust of crumbling walls and broken pottery. You could sense the spirit of death.

But, strangely, the photographs she had taken of the God of Renewal had not come out.

When the hour grew late, Emma placed the photos on her worktable and went in to bathe. That's where she was, soaking in the claw-footed tub, when Miguel arrived.

"I'm in the bathtub," she called out when she heard him come in. "Care to join me?"

He stuck his head in the doorway. "Don't tempt me." He shook his head. "I'm covered with dust. I'll wait till you've finished and have a shower."

"I won't be long. Why don't you fix us something cold to drink?"

"Fine. I'll bring the drinks in here."

Emma smiled as she lay back in the tub. When she finished she would go into the bedroom, close the blinds and wait for Miguel. They... She sat up. The refrigerator was in the darkroom. If he went in he would see the photographs. She didn't want him to, not until she explained why she had taken them.

"Miguel?" she called, but there was no answer.

She got out of the tub and, wrapping a towel around her body, hurried toward the darkroom. He was standing with his back to her, looking down at the photographs.

"I can explain," she said. "I—"

He turned and looked at her, an expression in his eyes she had never seen before.

"Listen..." She clutched at the towel that covered her nakedness. "I was going to tell you."

"Were you?"

"Of course."

He raised one eyebrow.

"I know you told me I couldn't go in the tomb because it was dangerous. But I..." She took another step into the room. "I need those photographs for my articles, Miguel."

"For your articles?" He shook his head. "Is that the only reason?"

Emma's eyes widened. "Of course. What do you mean?"

"It isn't because of your father?" He picked up the photographs of the bowls and urns. "You did say he collected artifacts, didn't you?"

"Yes, but..." She shook her head, trying to clear it, trying to make sense out of what he had just said. "My God..." She was stunned, unbelieving. "You can't actually think I took the photographs for my father. So that he..." She couldn't go on, could only stand there looking at him, her eyes wide with shock.

Miguel put the photographs back on her workbench. "I'd better go," he said.

"Not like this. Not until we straighten this out." She walked past him and picked them up. "Take them," she said. "Along with the negatives."

"Emma—"

"If you believe, after what we have meant to each other, that I would conspire to steal the artifacts, then take the photographs and leave."

Miguel hesitated. "Why did you do it?" he asked. "I told you when you asked to see the tomb that it wouldn't be open to the public for several months. Yet you went in anyway, without telling me."

"I'm sorry. I started thinking about the tomb and how much I wanted to see it. I only meant to photograph the entrance, but when I stepped inside I couldn't resist photographing the glyphs and the pottery." She lifted her shoulders. "I shouldn't have."

"No, you shouldn't have." He turned away. "You'd better get some clothes on."

She dressed quickly, but by the time she went out into the living room, Miguel had finished his drink. "I've got to leave," he said. "I have some work I need to do tonight."

"Don't you want to shower here?"

He shook his head, and avoiding her eyes, said, "No, I'd better go."

Emma took a sip of her drink.

"I'll be in touch. Tomorrow, probably."

Probably? She set her glass on the table by the window. "All right," she said.

He went to the door. He looked at her, then away. *"Hasta mañana,"* he said.

"Hasta..." But he had already closed the door.

She opened a can of soup for dinner, but when she tried to eat, she couldn't. Instead she sat by the window looking out at the street, wishing she had a television she could watch, whether in English or Spanish, to take her mind off all that she was feeling.

She didn't blame Miguel for being angry. She shouldn't have taken the photographs without his permission. But was what she had done so terrible? And how could he have possibly thought that she was spying for her father?

She remembered the conversation they'd had the very first time Miguel had taken her out to dinner, and the way he had looked when she told him her father collected artifacts. But that had been before he really knew her. How could he, after what they had shared, believe that she had taken the photographs for any other reason than to enhance her articles?

The hour grew late. She curled up on the sofa and tried to read. The words blurred. Finally, emotionally exhausted, she fell asleep. She didn't hear the car pull up, or the footsteps, or the light knock, but came awake when she heard him call her name.

Half waking, half sleeping she opened the door.

"Emma," he said. Then she was in his arms, holding him as he held her, weeping against his chest.

"Don't," he said. "*Querida,* don't. Please don't cry. I'm sorry I was angry."

"No," she wept. "It was my fault. I'm the one who's sorry. I shouldn't have gone into the tomb. I shouldn't have—"

He tilted her face to his and kissed her. "It's all right," he said against her lips. "Don't cry."

"You can take the photographs and the negatives, Miguel. Tear them up. Do anything you want with them."

"They're much too good to tear up." He wiped her tears away. "It's very late," he said. "Why weren't you in bed?"

"Because you weren't here."

"I'm here now." He kissed her again, and picking her up in his arms, carried her into the bedroom.

He was ashamed of having been suspicious of Emma. She was a professional photographer, doing a series of articles on archaeological sites. Of course she'd be interested in the newly uncovered tomb. Of course she would want to take photographs. The fact that her father collected artifacts had nothing to do with her.

He tried to tell himself that three days later when Emma said, "I had a telegram from my folks today."

They were having dinner at the restaurant on the quiet street. Miguel said, "Oh?" and took a sip of his wine. "How are they?"

"Fine." She picked up her wineglass, twisted the stem, and without drinking set it back down. "They're coming for a visit."

"Here? To Oaxaca?"

She cleared her throat. "Yes."

It has nothing to do with the tomb, he told himself. Or with the photographs. Or the fact that her father collects artifacts. They're her parents. They want to see her. But she would be going home in a few weeks. If they had wanted to see her, why hadn't they come before? Why now?

"They've been to Mexico before," she said, breaking in on his thoughts. "To Mexico City and to the Yucatán. But not to Oaxaca."

"I see."

"Dad wants to see Monte Alban and Mitla." She toyed with her fork. "It's a good opportunity. I mean, while I'm here."

"Yes, I suppose it is." The food stuck in his throat. It's just a coincidence that they're coming now, he tried to tell himself. It hasn't anything to do with the tomb.

"When are they arriving?" he asked.

"The day after tomorrow."

"We'll have to take them to dinner."

"That would be nice."

"Will they stay with you?"

Emma shook her head. "Dad wouldn't be comfortable. I've made a hotel reservation for them."

"How long do they plan to stay?"

"I'm not sure. For a week or ten days, probably."

Emma clasped her hands together under the table. She was not surprised at the way Miguel had responded to the news that her parents were coming to Oaxaca. She, too, felt ambivalent about their coming. She knew her father well enough to know that he would hate her small apartment, and he would certainly be curious about her relationship with Miguel. "He's a foreigner," she could almost hear him say. "How long have you known him? What does he do for a living?"

It would be different with her mother. Penelope would like Miguel and she'd like Oaxaca. In a recent letter she had written to say she had been reading everything she could find on Oaxaca and that she was planning to set a new children's book there.

"My mother wants to research a book while she's here," Emma said.

"She's a writer?"

"I told you about her. She writes children's books. It would be nice if she could meet Jose Antonio and Angelina." Emma smiled. "She'll very likely put them in her new book if she does."

This was happening too fast. Their relationship had been strained since the night he had discovered the photographs Emma had taken at the tomb. He had been angry that she had, but he had believed her when she said taking them had nothing to do with her father.

But now, less than a week after she'd gone into the tomb, her father was arriving in Oaxaca. Was it a co-incidence or had his earlier suspicions been justified.

He studied her face. She looked confused and un-happy, and for a moment he wanted to reach across the table and take her hand. He wanted to tell her that everything was all right, that he believed in her, that he knew she would never do anything that was less than honorable.

He wanted to, but he didn't.

James hadn't wanted to spend more than a day in Mexico City. "Too damn many people," he complained. "Everybody running around like a bunch of chickens with their heads cut off. Horns blowing, bells ringing. Smog thick enough to choke a horse. And the taxis! By God, they ought to sell life insurance to any-body who's fool enough to get into one."

"They're just trying to keep up with the traffic, dear." Penelope patted his hand. "We'll be in Oaxaca in another few minutes and you'll be able to relax."

"I won't relax till Emma's back where she be-longs." He glared at his wife as though it were her fault that their daughter was still in Mexico. "And why in the hell did she have to come in the summer? I hate hot weather."

"She came because she had an assignment to write the articles, James. You know that."

"She should've finished them by now. She's prob-ably hanging around because of that man she met, the archaeologist."

"Perhaps." Penelope smiled.

"You'd think there weren't any men in Denver. Why in the hell she had to come all the way to southern Mexico to find a man is beyond my comprehension."

"I know that, dear."

James shot her a glance, but before he could answer, she said, "Look, we're almost there. You can see the city. Fasten your seat belt, James. We're going to land."

Miguel had offered to go to the airport with Emma, but she'd said, "No, you're busy. You'll meet my parents at dinner tonight."

He wasn't looking forward to it, but he would go because of Emma, and because he wanted to know more about her father. He didn't think much of anybody who collected artifacts, who took them out of the country they belonged in, but he would try to reserve judgment until after he had met James Pilgrim.

He spent a frustrating day at Monte Alban, most of it in the tomb. One of his helpers, Felipe, a young archaeological student from the University of Mexico who was working with Miguel that summer, had called his attention to something that struck him as strange.

"I could swear that urn in the corner wasn't broken when I left yesterday," he said. "I'd seen that it was chipped, and I remember thinking that I'd better handle it carefully." Felipe got down on his hands and knees. "And look, Señor Rivas, some of the pieces of pottery are crushed."

Miguel knelt beside Felipe. He leaned down and, focusing his flashlight carefully, examined the dirt floor of the tomb. Felipe was right, the place had been disturbed. Someone had been here during the night.

Cursing under his breath, he got to his feet. Where in the hell had the guards been last night? He'd hired two of them so that nothing like this would happen. Damn it to hell, someone had gotten into the tomb. Someone was after the artifacts.

He stayed until both relief guards arrived at six. "I know it's difficult to patrol the whole area," he said. "I want one of you on patrol and I want one of you here at the tomb all night. Is that clear?"

They looked at each other. "Sure, boss," one of them said. "Either Salvador or I will stay right here. I don't know how anybody could have got past us, but it won't happen again. That's a promise."

"It damn well had better be," Miguel had retorted.

It was after six when he left the site, and almost eight before he knocked at the door of Emma's apartment.

"I was worried," she said when she let him in. "I thought something had happened to you."

Miguel shook his head. "There was a problem out at the site."

She chewed her bottom lip. "Dad hates to eat late. We'd better go."

"First things first." He drew her into his arms and kissed her.

For a moment her lips parted under his, then she stepped back and, sounding nervous, said, "You've got a smudge of lipstick on your mouth. Let me wipe it off."

He stood still while she took a tissue out of her bag and wiped his mouth. "Take it easy," he said.

She took a deep breath. "Okay." She shrugged. "So I'm nervous."

"Your parents can't be that bad."

"You haven't met my father." She forced a smile, and taking a deep breath, said, "All right. Let's go."

Her parents were waiting for them in the lobby of their hotel.

"*Been* waiting for forty-five minutes," her father said.

He was a tall, florid-faced man in his early sixties. He had a generous shock of gray hair, gray eyebrows, and eyes that were as green as Emma's. His wife, a delicate woman with short curly hair and a pink-and-white complexion, came barely to his shoulder.

"I'm sorry we're late," Miguel said. "It's my fault. We had a problem out at the site today." He offered his hand. "I'm Miguel Rivas, Señor Pilgrim. Welcome to Oaxaca." He smiled at Penelope. "I hope you had a good flight, *Señora.*"

"It was spectacular," Penelope said.

James looked at his watch. "Long past time for dinner," he muttered.

"Not in Mexico." Emma linked her arm through his. "I think you'll enjoy the restaurant. It's a favorite of ours."

Her father raised his eyebrows, but before he could make a comment, Miguel said, "We can walk to the restaurant. It's only a couple of blocks from the *zocalo.*"

"The central plaza," Penelope said. "Like the one in Mexico City."

"But a lot more colorful, Señora Pilgrim."

"Penelope," she said. "Or Penny. That's what my friends call me."

Miguel smiled, liking her. She was, as Emma had once told him, a small butterfly of a woman. Her bright blond hair curled about her face in a becoming fashion. Her blue eyes were alive with excitement and curiosity.

She loved the *zocalo,* and when James impatiently hurried her on, she looked at Miguel and said, "But we can come back after dinner, can't we?"

"*Por supuesto,* of course."

The restaurant was almost full when they entered, but Miguel had made a reservation and they were led to a table near the window. When they were seated, he ordered champagne. "To celebrate your being here," he said.

Penelope beamed at him. "That's nice, Miguel. Thank you." She looked around the restaurant, a pleased smile on her face, and said, "Isn't this pretty? And doesn't everything smell good?"

"I hope you like the food. The chicken in mole sauce is their speciality and I can recommend it."

"Then that's what I'll have."

"Not me," James said. "I'll have steak. Well done."

Penelope chattered on all through dinner. She was interested in everything. How did they make mole? she wanted to know. Was there really chocolate in it? Was it true there were still so many Indian tribes in the state of Oaxaca? She couldn't wait to see all the arts-and-crafts stores.

"Emma told me you have two children." She smiled at Miguel. "I'd love to meet them."

"I'll make sure that you do."

"You're a divorced man?" James asked.

"No, Dad," Emma said. "Miguel's wife died when his little girl was born."

"I'm so sorry." Penelope covered his hand with hers. "It must be difficult for you, trying to raise them all alone."

"They live with my mother." He looked across the table at Emma. "We could drive out this weekend," he said.

"And have a picnic." Penelope clapped her hands. "Wouldn't that be fun, James?"

Emma's father looked at his wife over the top of his black horn-rimmed glasses. "A barrel of laughs," he said.

Penelope's cheeks got red and she looked down at her plate. "I'm sure it will be nice, Miguel. I'm looking forward to meeting your children."

For a while after that the conversation was stilted. It was not until they were served their after-dinner coffee that James turned to Miguel. "I understand you're working out at Monte Alban. Emma's told me about the tomb you've recently uncovered. I'd like to take a look at it."

"Emma told you about the tomb?" Miguel glanced at her, then said, "I'm afraid the tomb isn't open to the public yet."

"But I'm a collector," James said. "I've seen just about every archaeological site in the world. Even went on digs while I was in college, one summer down in Honduras, another in Peru. Brought back a ceramic pot from there that's at least a thousand years old." He took a gulp of his coffee. "When Penny and

I were in Egypt I bought a magnificent piece, a carved mask imbedded with jade that goes back to the time of the pharaohs.''

Miguel crushed his linen napkin. ''Things like that belong to the country they're found in,'' he said stiffly.

''They belong to whoever has them in his possession,'' James retorted.

''The piece you bought in Egypt might have been a fake.''

''Nonsense! I bought it from a reputable dealer, a man who someone I know in New York often deals with.''

''But artifacts aren't supposed to be taken out of the country,'' Miguel said as calmly as he could. ''It's a dangerous thing to do, Señor Pilgrim. And it's a criminal offense.''

James exploded. ''Are you trying to tell me I'm a criminal?''

''Perhaps you weren't aware of the law, but it's pretty much universal now. Not long ago an American in Turkey was arrested and put in prison. He had bought what he thought was a copy of an urn from a street peddler. But it wasn't a copy, it was an original. The police stopped him as he was getting on the plane.''

Miguel leaned forward in his chair. ''Our laws here in Mexico are as strict as they are in Turkey. Our history belongs to us and we're determined to protect it.''

''In my opinion artifacts belong where everybody can see them,'' James said. ''Your Museum of Anthropology is a wonderful place, but so is the Metropolitan Museum in New York. That's where I'd like to see some of the stuff from Mexico—right out where everybody can see it."

Stuff? Miguel took a deep breath, and knowing he had to get out of here before he said something he'd be sorry for, he signaled for the check.

"It's late," he said to Emma. "I'm sure your mother and father are tired from their trip."

"Yes." She bit her lip and looked from him to her father as though to say, *I'm sorry. I wanted this to work out. I wanted you to like each other.*

And because of that look, because of the appeal in her eyes, Miguel found himself saying, "If you'd like to go out to Monte Alban tomorrow, Señor Pilgrim, I'd be happy to show you around."

James's eyes widened, then he grinned. "Hell, yes, I'd like to go!"

"Is seven too early? I could take you in before the tourists arrive and before it gets too hot."

"Seven's fine." James drummed the table with his fingers. "Nice of you to offer, Rivas. I appreciate it."

Emma walked with her father on the way back to the hotel, Miguel with her mother. Miguel gallantly bought each woman a bouquet of gardenias, and when they arrived back at the hotel, Penelope stood on her tiptoes and kissed his cheek.

"It was a wonderful dinner, Miguel. Thank you."

"My pleasure." He offered his hand to James. "I'll see you in the morning," he said.

"I'll be ready."

Emma kissed both her parents. She told her mother she would meet her in the morning for breakfast and told her father to enjoy his day. Then, arm in arm, she and Miguel walked the few blocks back to her apartment.

"Well?" she asked when they were alone.

"Well what?"

"How did you like my parents?"

"Your mother is like a *muñeca*," he said. "Just like a little doll. But your father..." He shook his head. "He's tough, Emma."

"I know he is, Miguel. But when you get to know him you find the soft spots. It's hard for him to show that side of himself, but believe me, it's there." She hesitated. "About the tomb," she said. "I told him about it after you told me. The first time, I mean. When we first met. I didn't want you to think that I told him after I went into the tomb. I didn't."

"I didn't think you had."

Which wasn't really true. That's exactly what he'd thought, if even for a moment. He didn't like being suspicious of Emma; didn't want to be, because he didn't think he could stand it if she wasn't everything she seemed to be.

And because he didn't want to think about it, he took her hand and led her into the bedroom. They made love and afterward he held her until she went to sleep. Only then did he allow himself to think about her father, and wonder at the real reason James Pilgrim had come to Oaxaca.

Chapter 12

James was a great deal more knowledgeable than Miguel had expected him to be. His questions were intelligent and his appreciation of the ancient city was obvious. When he first looked down on the site, he said, "I've seen photographs of Monte Alban, but I never dreamed it would be this magnificent. It's an archaeological wonder."

"Yes, it is." Miguel turned his gaze from the site of the city to the mountains that surrounded it. It had rained during the night and the sky was a clean, clear blue for as far as he could see. Later on it would be hot, but this morning the air was refreshingly cool.

"Think what it must have been like to have discovered this—the first modern man that did, I mean. Can you imagine him coming up over the rise of land and seeing it all laid out in front of him?" James pointed toward the ball court. "Incredible," he said, shaking his head in wonder. "Incredible."

Miguel had not liked Emma's father last night. He was not sure he liked him now, but he found as he began showing James around the site that some of his animosity began to fade. Irascible though James Pilgrim might be, his appreciation of this archaeological zone was real.

Because it was, and because he thought it might be a good idea to know more about Emma's father, and yes, to keep an eye on him, Miguel found himself saying, "The new tomb isn't open to the public, but if you'd like to see it I'll show it to you."

"If I'd like to see it!" James actually smiled. "My God, yes. Of course I'd like to see it."

They crossed the grassy plain together. As they approached the tomb, Miguel saluted the guard. "Any problems?" he asked.

"No, Señor Rivas." The guard rested a hand on the revolver strapped at his waist. "Anybody who tries to pass without permission will have me and *mi amigo* here to deal with. It is the same with the guards at night. Believe me, Señor Rivas, we are armed and ready."

Miguel could not believe that a man like James Pilgrim would stoop to stealing, but he did believe that he wasn't above buying artifacts from someone who would. It did no harm to let James know that the tomb was well guarded.

Pilgrim's interest in the tomb was sincere. His appreciation was profound, almost reverent. When he asked if he could return the following day to either work in the tomb or help in cleaning what was taken out, Miguel, after a moment's hesitation, said, "Yes, if you want to. It's hard and dirty work, though."

"It's something I'd really like to do, Señor Rivas."

"Miguel, Señor Pilgrim."

"Call me James."

Miguel nodded, and a truce of sorts was declared.

The following morning the two of them drove out to the site together. All that day James Pilgrim worked in the tomb with Miguel and young Felipe. He dusted the walls inch by inch with a small soft brush. On his hands and knees he sifted through dirt and pieces of broken pottery. When they broke for lunch, Miguel expected him to call it quits. But he didn't. He wiped a hand across his sweaty face and said, "I haven't enjoyed myself this much in years. It's bloody wonderful, isn't it?"

By the time he returned to the hotel he was sweat-stained and dirty. He sang, "Oh, give me a man who's a stouthearted man," while he showered, and when he came out of the bathroom with a towel wrapped around his body, he grinned at his wife and said, "I had one hell of a good day."

"I'm so glad, dear."

"What did you and Emma do?"

"We shopped. I bought a few pieces of black pottery and this." She turned around slowly, showing off a hot pink ruffled dress. "How do you like it?"

James looked her up and down. "It'll do," he said. "Maybe I'd like it better off than on."

Penelope's bright blue eyes widened. "You don't like it?"

"I didn't say that. I said I'd like it better off, at least for a little while."

"Oh?" She looked startled. "Oh!"

He put a finger under her chin and lifted her face for a kiss. "The dress is much too nice to wrinkle, Pretty Penny."

"You haven't called me that for a long time, James."

"Too long." He kissed her again, and when she took the hot pink dress off he picked her up and carried her to the bed.

When Miguel telephoned to tell his mother that he and Emma wanted to take the children on a picnic with her parents, he added, "I'd like you to come along, Mother."

"Why should I? I don't know those people and neither do the children. I can't imagine why you would want to take them out with complete strangers."

"They're Emma's parents," he said patiently. "I really thought you might enjoy meeting them."

"I doubt that very much." She sighed her martyred sigh. "What time do you want me to have the children ready?" she asked.

"Ten, if that's not too early."

"Ten," she said. "Goodbye."

Jose Antonio and Angelina ran down the steps as soon as the car pulled up in front of the house. They hugged Emma and Miguel, and when Emma introduced them to her parents, Jose Antonio shook hands with both her father and mother.

But Angelina hung back, thumb in her mouth, looking down at her shoes. Emma picked her up. In careful Spanish she said, "This is my mother, Angelina. And this is my father. They came all the way from the United States to meet you and Jose."

"We certainly did." And to Emma's surprise, her mother said, "*Tu vestido es muy bonito.* Your dress is very pretty." She smiled warmly. "*Y tú también,* and so are you."

Angelina took her thumb out of her mouth. "*Mucho gusto,*" she whispered, and offered her cheek for a kiss.

Miguel introduced James and Penelope to his mother. Maria Leticia, regally polite, invited them in for coffee. Miguel was about to refuse, but before he could, Penelope said, "Thank you, Mrs. Rivas. That would be real nice." And when she saw the roses that grew near the steps, she said, "Just look at these. Aren't they beautiful! I love roses, but I have a terrible time trying to grow them. I don't know whether I overwater or underwater. They never look like these do."

"You must fertilize them."

"I do, with whatever it is I buy at the nursery."

"Chemicals!" Maria Leticia shook her head. "You must use the excrement from goats if you want roses like this."

"From goats." Penelope looked thoughtful. "Thank you for telling me that, Mrs. Rivas. I'll certainly try it when I get back home to Denver."

For the first time since they had arrived, Maria Leticia smiled.

The two women chatted, Penelope in her slow but careful Spanish, while Hortensia served coffee and hot buttered cinnamon rolls. When it was time to leave, Penelope shook hands with Miguel's mother. "I'm sorry you can't come with us today," she said. And just for a moment, Maria Leticia looked sorry, too.

"I didn't know you spoke Spanish," Emma said to her mother once they were in the car. "When did you learn?"

"I started taking classes right after you left for Mexico. I had a hunch your father and I might visit you and that very likely I'd want to set a book here. It seemed to me if I was going to, I needed to speak the language. When I started studying I discovered I liked it, so I hired a private tutor. For the last three weeks he's been coming to the house three times a week." She beamed a smile toward the two children, and to Emma said, "I'm still not very good, but being here, especially with the children, will help a lot."

Miguel took his eyes off the road long enough to look at James and say, "You have a very nice wife, *Señor*."

"Damned if I don't know it." James reached around to the back seat and patted Penelope's hand. "You're a wonder, girl," he said.

They returned to the place by the stream where they had picnicked before. The day was warm. Wildflowers grew in scattered abandon and the sun shone through the willow trees. Jose Antonio asked if it would be all right if he and Angelina went wading.

"Yes," Miguel said. "But stay where we can see you."

"Emma and I will go with them." Penelope turned to her daughter. "Yes?"

"Yes," Emma said with a laugh, and hand in hand, mother and daughter went to join the children.

The two men leaned back against the wide trunk of a tree and looked toward the stream. Water splashed in the sunshine, and in the shimmering incandescent light it seemed to Miguel that everything blurred together in a bright rainbow of colors: the yellow of Jose Antonio's shirt, Angelina's red pinafore, Emma's blue sundress and the hot pink gown Penelope wore.

"Butterflies," James said, breaking in on his thoughts. "That's what they look like, don't they?" He shifted toward Miguel. "That's how I've always seen Penny. But I never thought of Emma that way. She's always been more like me than her mother. Has her feet on the ground, and isn't given to flights of fancy the way her mother is."

Just at that moment Emma picked Angelina up and held her high above her head. Drops of water seemed to hang suspended from the little girl's bare feet. She burst into delighted giggles and so did Emma.

"Emma's changed," James said. "I think you're responsible."

"I'm not sure I know what you mean."

"Yes, you do."

"You don't like the change?"

"I didn't say that. What I'm wondering is where it's going, whatever it is that's between you and my daughter. I've seen the way you look at each other so don't try to tell me that something isn't going on."

"I won't."

James's green eyes, so like Emma's, shot sparks of fire. "Emma isn't a frivolous woman, Rivas. She takes things seriously, her work as well as her personal relationships."

"I'd never do anything to hurt her," Miguel said. "I respect the way you feel, James, but what is between us is between *us*."

"She's my daughter and I—"

"I'm hungry." Jose Antonio plopped down on the grass beside them. "When are we going to eat?"

Miguel reached out and ruffled his son's hair. "Just as soon as we can get the women out of the water. Why don't you go get them?"

"Bien." With a yip, Jose ran back to the stream, shouting, "It's time to eat! Hurry up, I'm hungry!"

In a quiet voice, Miguel said, "Emma is your daughter, James, but she's not a little girl. She's a woman and she can make her own decisions. I don't know what will happen between us. There are problems that have to be worked out. But they are our problems."

"You hurt her and I'll come back to Oaxaca and break your neck."

"If I do you'll be entitled."

They ate the picnic Emma and Penelope had prepared. If the two women realized there was tension between the two men, they didn't speak of it. When they finished eating, Jose Antonio went back to the stream.

Penelope took Angelina's hand and said, "Would you like me to tell you a story, *niña?*" And when Angelina nodded, Penelope settled down with her beneath one of the pepper trees. "Once upon a time," she began, and in a little while, with her head on Penelope's lap, the little girl went to sleep.

"They're wonderful children, Emma," Penelope said when Emma came to sit beside them. "And from what I've seen of Miguel, he's an exceptional man."

"Yes, he is. I like him a lot, Mama."

"I rather suspected you did." Penelope smiled gently at her daughter. "Is there anything you want to tell me, Emma?"

"Only that—that I love him."

"I knew that the first time I saw the two of you together." She stroked the back of Emma's hand. "Does he love you, my dear?"

"I don't know. I tell myself he does or he couldn't be the way he is."

"He hasn't said anything?"

Emma shook her head.

"It hasn't been very long. Give it time."

"I don't have time. I'll be leaving in another few weeks."

"Does Miguel know how you feel?"

"I'm not sure. He knows I care about him, but of course I've never..." Emma shook her head. "I've never told him that I love him."

"Maybe you should."

Emma looked startled. "I couldn't do that. I mean, if he doesn't tell me—"

"If he doesn't tell you first?" Penelope shook her head. "You're always so sensible, Emma. You always want to think things through and weigh every possibility before you act. When you were only five or six I remember thinking that you were far more serious about everything than I was. I'd read you stories about faeries or beautiful princesses in faraway lands, and you'd say, "That's just not possible, Mama.""

Emma stiffened. "I couldn't have been that bad."

"You weren't bad at all," her mother said. "You never talked back or made a mess. You picked up your toys and cleaned your room. You were a model child." Penelope sighed. "You were always your father's daughter," she said with a touch of sadness. "And I wanted so much for you to be mine."

"But I am yours." Hot tears stung Emma's eyes. "Mama, I am."

"If you were you wouldn't be afraid to tell Miguel that you love him." She turned to look toward her husband, who stood talking to Miguel. "I wasn't afraid to tell your father how I felt about him."

"What happened when you did?"

Penelope laughed. "He was shocked right down to his argyle socks. Then he harrumphed and said, 'Me, too.' I said, 'What does that mean?' He harrumphed a couple more times but finally said, 'Well, by God, so do I. Love you, I mean.'"

Her eyes warm with love, Penelope said, "What difference does it make who says it first? Loving isn't something to be ashamed of, Emma. Be proud that you love Miguel."

"But if he doesn't love me back?"

"I've seen the way he looks at you, Emma. I'm sure he does."

"We're very different."

"As different as your father and I are?" Laughter bubbled on Penelope's lips. "Darling, you and Miguel may be from different countries, but your father and I are from different planets."

Emma smiled, but before she could answer, a crash of thunder split the air and she felt the first splatter of rain on her face. "A storm is coming," she said. "We'd better get the things together before it gets worse."

It got worse very quickly. Penelope woke Angelina while Emma hurried to gather up the things from the picnic. Miguel ran to help her, but before he could reach her the sky opened up and rain poured down. A fierce roll of thunder shook the ground, and a sudden wind pulled at the picnic cloth and overturned the glasses.

"You and your mother and father get to the car," Miguel shouted over the roar of the wind. "I'll take care of things."

They were all soaked by now and the rain was coming down so hard it was difficult to see. A bolt of lightning flashed through the trees. Angelina buried her face against Penelope's shoulder and started to cry.

"Take care of the children," James said. "Miguel and I will..." He stopped. "Where's the boy?"

"He went wading. He..." The color drained from Miguel's face. *"¡Ay Dios!"* he cried, and ran toward the stream.

Emma started after him but her father grabbed her arm. "I'll go," he said, and sprinted after Miguel.

The rain beat down in blinding silver sheets. Branches from the willow and pepper trees slapped at Miguel's face. Waist-high water swirled hard and fast through the arroyo.

"Jose Antonio!" he cried. "Joselito! Where are you?"

He stopped for a moment, heart beating hard against his ribs, mouth dry with fear. James caught up with him. The older man's gray hair was slicked flat against his head and rain dripped down his face.

"Flash flood," Miguel said, remembering other storms, the terrible danger in dry desert places, when the floodwaters swept everything away and campers caught in them drowned.

"I'll take this side of the stream, you take the other," James said. Miguel waded into the churning water and crossed the stream.

One on each side, the two of them ran along the arroyo, battling the wind and rain. Both of them kept crying out, "Jose Antonio! Jose Antonio!"

Miguel ran on, almost crazy with fear. Where was his boy? Oh, God! Where was his son?

A branch slammed hard against his head, causing him to stagger. Rain and blood ran down over his forehead. He heard the cry of the wind, then above it another cry. "Jose!" he shouted. "Joselito!"

He shaded his eyes, frantically searching the trees and the water, and finally saw his son clinging to a branch of a pepper tree. Water swirled around his feet, coming closer every minute.

"Hang on," Miguel cried. "I'm coming."

He slipped from the bank into the water, struggling hard to keep his footing. There was a flash of orange lightning; he saw Jose's white, frightened face and fought his way to the tree. The water was rising. In another minute it would reach his son.

Half swimming, half walking, Miguel made his way to the tree and reached up for Jose. "I've got you," he cried. "Let go."

For a moment Jose only looked at him, his face frozen with fear, then he said, *"Papá!"* and reached out to him.

Miguel pulled the boy into his arms and Jose grabbed him around the neck. "I've got you," Miguel cried. "Hang on, Jose. Hang on, Joselito."

He started toward the bank, but the swirl of the water was against him. He tried to grasp at a branch but it was beyond his reach. Jose Antonio's arms tightened around his neck. Miguel staggered, heard the boy gasp in fright, and regained his footing.

A cry came from the other side of the stream, and through the torrent of rushing water Miguel saw James, waist deep in water. James swung his arm back and a rope came sailing out over the water. Miguel reached for it, and missed.

James pulled the rope back. Through the driving rain Miguel saw the desperation on James's face, and the fear as he tried again. This time the rope sailed over Miguel's head. He reached up and grabbed it, but the reaching had thrown him off balance. He lost his footing, struggled to regain it and fell.

Dark water swirled over his head. Jose! his mind screamed. Jose!

He found his footing and fought his way to the surface. He still had hold of the rope and Jose Antonio still had hold of him. He tied the rope around his waist, and with one hand on it and the other steadying Jose, he started toward the safety of the other shore. Once again he lost his footing. If it hadn't been for the rope, he and Jose would have been swept away in the current.

Ten yards, eight. Closer and yet closer they came, struggling through the terrible force of the water. On toward James, who was braced against the shore, pulling them forward. Miguel was not even aware that he said his son's name over and over because the sound of it gave him strength.

Firmer footing. James reaching out to him, grabbing Jose Antonio, setting the boy safely on the shore. Reaching for Miguel's hand, pulling him up those last few feet.

On his hands and knees on the bank, Miguel fought for breath. Jose Antonio was beside him, pale and wet and frightened, but alive. *Gracias a Dios*, alive. He pulled his son into his arms, rocking him closely, whispering his name over and over again.

James put a hand on Miguel's shoulder. "We've got to get him to shelter," he shouted above the roar of the wind.

Miguel stood. He picked up his son, and with James steadying him, headed for the car. He saw Emma running through the rain toward them, heard her cry, "Miguel! Miguel!"

She saw the blood running down his forehead, saw her father, and Jose Antonio's pale, frightened face. She put an arm around Miguel's shoulders, and the three of them, with the child, fought their way to the car.

The *Hospital Civil* was small and ill equipped, but the two doctors there were efficient. One of them, who looked to be no more than twenty-one or twenty-two, took Jose Antonio from Miguel's arms and laid him on an examining table. A nurse stripped off the boy's wet clothing and covered him with a warm blanket. Another nurse took Jose's blood pressure. A different doctor checked his pulse and respiration. He shone a light in Jose's eyes and ran a hand carefully over the boy's head. "What's your name, son?" he asked.

"Jose..." The boy was shivering so violently he could barely speak. "Jose Antonio," he managed to say.

"Can you tell me what day it is?"

"*Sá-sábado.*"

"Very good." The doctor ran his hands down Jose Antonio's body, noting the cuts and scratches on the boy's arms and legs. "Does anything hurt?" he asked.

"I don't—don't think so." Jose's teeth were chattering, his fingers tinged with blue.

"*Un suero,*" the doctor said. "Fix an IV."

"What is it?" Miguel's voice was strained with fear. "What's the matter?"

"The boy has had a shock. The IV will help stabilize him." The doctor looked more closely at Miguel. "Sit down, *señor,*" he said. "We'll attend to your cut in a moment."

"I'm all right," Miguel protested.

James took his arm. "The doctor's right," he said. "You'd better sit down."

"No, I..." His vision blurred. He took a deep breath to steady himself and it cleared. "James," he said. "If it hadn't been for you—"

"You'd have made it," James told him.

"Maybe." But Miguel knew that if James hadn't been there, if he hadn't had sense enough to run back to the car for the rope, he might not have. Neither he nor Jose Antonio.

He couldn't speak then, but he held out his hand. James grasped it. They looked at each other, both with the knowledge of how close it had been.

The nurses put Jose Antonio to bed. They insisted on cleaning Miguel's wound, and when they had bandaged his head, he pulled up a chair and sat beside his son.

Emma stood beside him. "We've got to take Angelina home," she said. "When she realized Jose Antonio was missing she became hysterical. She's still terribly upset and she's shaking with cold. We've got to get her into dry clothes."

Miguel nodded. "You, too. And your mother and father." He shook his head. "If it hadn't been for him, Emma..." He swallowed hard, unable to go on.

"I know," she said. "I know."

He reached into his pocket and took out his keys. "You can find your way?"

Emma nodded. She tightened her hand on his shoulder. "I'll come back," she promised. "Just as soon as I can."

He looked at her. "Yes," he said. "Please return. I—I need you, Emma." Then he turned again to his son.

At the door of the room she looked back. Miguel was leaning over the bed. He stroked the dark hair on Jose Antonio's pale forehead. *"Mi niño,"* he whispered. "My son."

Chapter 13

After the initial shock of finding Emma, her parents and Angelina all dripping wet at her front door, Maria Leticia recovered enough to say, "*¡Dios Mio! ¿Qué pasa?* Come in, come in." She motioned them inside, then her dark eyes grew wide and she asked, "Where are Miguel and Jose Antonio?"

Penelope put a reassuring hand on her arm. "They're all right," she said quickly. "The storm caught us by surprise while Jose Antonio was wading. The arroyo rose and—and there was a little difficulty. But they're both all right. Miguel thought it best to take Jose Antonio to the hospital, and the doctors there suggested he spend the night so they could keep an eye on him."

"Jose Antonio is in the hospital?" Hands clutched to her bosom, Maria Leticia looked from Penelope to Emma, unable for a moment to speak.

"Miguel wanted to stay with him," Emma said. "Jose was frightened but he wasn't hurt." She tightened her arms around the little girl shivering in her arms. "Angelina needs a warm bath, *señora,* and something hot to drink. If you'll tell me where to take her—"

"The bathroom across the corridor from her room." Maria Leticia straightened her shoulders. "I'll make hot chocolate. And soup. You'll need dry clothes," she said.

The three Americans, with Angelina clinging to Emma, followed Miguel's mother down the hall. She took clothes from her closet for Emma and Penelope to wear, and told James where Miguel's room was.

"His jeans won't fit you," she said, "but his pajamas and robe will." Her mouth was drawn into a tight, firm line. Her spine was as rigid as her expression. She started back the way they had come, then paused to say, "I'll see to the soup."

Emma went to her. "Miguel and Jose Antonio really are all right," she said gently. "I'd tell you if they weren't."

Maria Leticia's mouth trembled. "There was no reason for the picnic. There wouldn't have been one— they wouldn't have gone—if it hadn't been for you. It's your fault. Because of you..." She shook her head, then turned and left the room.

"She's just upset," Penelope said, looking concerned. "I'm sure she didn't mean to say that." She patted Emma's arm. "You go ahead and take care of Angelina. Your father and I will be just fine."

Emma took the clothes Maria Leticia had given her and went down the hall to Angelina's room. In the bathroom across from it she ran a tub of hot water, and stripping the wet clothes off the child, helped her into the tub. Angelina was shivering and her eyes were too big for her face.

"Jose Antonio is going to be all right," Emma said as she began to bathe the little girl. "The doctors just wanted him to stay at the hospital because he had a bad scare and he was so cold. Your *papá* is with him, and in a little while I'm going back to the hospital to make sure he and Jose are all right."

Angelina's chin wobbled. "I want to go with you," she said with a sniff.

"I think it's better if you stay here, sweetheart." Emma soaped Angelina's back. "You'll have some soup and a nice cup of hot chocolate, and then my mother will tuck you into bed and tell you a story. Would you like that?"

Angelina sniffed again, but she nodded and said, "*Sí*, Emma."

By the time she took the child out of the tub and helped her into her nightgown, Emma herself was shivering with cold. "You go on into the kitchen," she said. "I'm going to have a bath, too. I'll be there in just a little while." She kissed Angelina's cheek. "It's going to be all right, *niña*," she said. "Your *papá* and Jose Antonio are going to be fine, I promise you." She patted Angelina's bottom. "Now run along to the kitchen."

She went back to the bathroom, and when she had taken off her wet clothes, got into the tub of hot water and sank into it up to her chin. She was shaking with cold and reaction now that she was alone, and reliving again that terrible moment when they had discovered that Jose Antonio was missing. She closed her eyes, remembering the look on Miguel's face as he'd turned to run for the arroyo. And her own fear, for the boy and for him.

The first time they had come to Dos Santos she had asked him why he saw his children so infrequently. He'd had no answer to her question and she had thought him uncaring. But he did care; she knew that now. She had seen the anguish on his face when he returned to the car cradling his son in his arms. And the love when he leaned over the small, pale boy in the hospital.

She had judged him without knowing the reasons why he couldn't keep his children with him. Now she was deeply sorry that she had.

She wondered then about the girl he had married when he was seventeen, the girl who became the woman who had given him Jose Antonio and Angelina. Had he loved her? Emma sighed and closed her eyes. That girl had been his first love. He had lain with her night after night, had made love with her hundreds of times. Of course he had loved her. But had his love for Yolanda been so deep and so strong that there could never be room in his heart for another woman? Would he forever cling to the memory of his dead wife?

With a sigh Emma got out of the tub and dressed in the long-sleeved blouse and black skirt that Maria Leticia had given her. She thought of the words the Mexican woman had said about the accident being her fault. And told herself, as her mother had, that Miguel's mother had been upset, that she hadn't meant what she'd said.

The skirt came to her ankles; the blouse drooped on her shoulders. But Emma had no choice—her own clothes were wet. Her sandals were wet, too, but they were all she had. She had to wear them.

The idea of going into the kitchen to face Maria Leticia was not an appealing one. She would drink a cup of hot chocolate, then would take her parents back to the city and return to the hospital.

But when Emma told her parents she would take them to Oaxaca as soon as they were ready, her father shook his head.

"Señora Rivas has invited us to stay here," he said. "The weather is still bad, so it seems like a good idea." He studied Emma over the rim of his cup. "You're going back to the hospital?"

"Yes, I want to be with Miguel." She looked across the table. She did not like Maria Leticia and it was obvious the woman didn't like her. But she was Miguel's mother, and because she was, Emma said, "Perhaps you would like to come with me, *señora*."

For a moment Maria Leticia looked startled. "No," she said, "but—but thank you for asking." Her lips pursed and a muscle in her cheek jumped. "I'm sorry for what I said earlier. I didn't mean it. It wasn't your fault. I apologize."

The words had come with difficulty and Emma accepted them. "I understand how upset you were," she said. "I'm sure Jose Antonio is fine, but either Miguel or I will call from the hospital."

"Are you going to stay all night?" Penelope asked.

Emma nodded. "I want to be there for Miguel," she said in English.

She ate her soup and drank the cup of steaming chocolate, then pushed her chair back.

"It's dark and it's still raining." James got up and put his arms around her. "Be careful driving, honey, and call us as soon as you get there so we know you're all right."

"I will." Emma hugged him. She gave Angelina a squeeze and kissed her mother's cheek.

"The air is cool." Maria Leticia shoved her chair back. "I'll get you a rebozo." She hurried out of the room and came back with the Mexican shawl. "Put this on," she said.

"*Gracias.*" Emma rested her hand on Maria Leticia's shoulder. "Try not to worry, *señora*. I'm sure Jose is going to be just fine."

There was a slight trembling of the older woman's mouth. She handed Emma a plastic shopping bag and said, "There's a thermos of soup and one of coffee, as well as sandwiches and fruit. I've put in a change of clothes for Jose Antonio and for Miguel, too." With a visible effort she added, "I'm glad you're going back to the hospital. It will help Miguel if you are with him tonight."

It took more than an hour for Emma to reach the small hospital. There were no lights on the road and it was difficult to see where she was going. Even more difficult to see the potholes that made driving so hazardous.

When she pulled into the muddy parking space at the side of the hospital, Emma put the black rebozo over her head and, taking the plastic shopping bag, hurried from the car.

A nurse nodded to her when she entered. From a room somewhere down the hall babies were crying. "Premies," the nurse explained. "Twin girls that came early." She shook her head. "We're doing our best to save them but we don't have the equipment of a bigger hospital."

Another nurse was typing reports at a manual typewriter. The small radio next to her was tuned to a rock station. Elvis Presley was singing "Blue Suede Shoes." A bored-looking young man lounged against an examining table, cigarette dangling from his lips, a damp mop and a bucket of dirty water at his side.

Emma went past him to the room where they had taken Jose Antonio earlier. The sound of Elvis's voice followed her.

She stood in the doorway of the room. Jose Antonio, the IV still hooked up to his arm, looked pale and quiet. Miguel sat beside him, holding his hand.

"Miguel?" she said softly, so as not to waken the sleeping child.

He turned and looked at her, too startled for a moment to answer. Dressed all in black, with the rebozo over her head, she looked like a Mexican woman from a small village. It came to him that this was the way his grandmother Rosa had looked, the way he remembered her and always thought of her. If Emma had been born in one of the small *pueblitos* nearby, she might have looked exactly like this. If she had, she would have been the passive and dutiful wife of a poor farmer and had six or seven children by now. The thought made him smile; he couldn't imagine Emma ever being passive about anything.

He stood and walked over to her. "Thank you for coming," he said.

"I wanted to be here." She looked at the sleeping boy. "How is he?" she asked.

"Better. The doctor checked on him a little while ago." He looked at the plastic bag. "Is that something to eat?"

"Hot soup and sandwiches and coffee. And clothes for you and Jose Antonio. Your mother sent it."

"Is she all right?"

Emma nodded. "She was alarmed when we arrived without you or Jose. She's still worried, of course, but yes, she's fine. My mother and father are going to stay with her tonight."

He breathed a sigh of relief. "And Angelina?"

"She was very frightened, Miguel, but she's all right. Mother will tuck her in and read her a story."

Emma took the rebozo off. "I told your mother that either you or I would call her. Why don't you go ahead? Call her and then change into the dry clothes. I'll stay with Jose Antonio."

He rested a hand on her shoulder. He wanted to tell her how grateful he was that she had come back, how much it meant to him to have her here. He touched the side of her face and said, "Thank you, Emma. Thank you for coming."

He asked the nurse who was typing records if he could use the phone at her desk. She said yes, and turned the blaring radio down.

His mother answered on the second ring. "Miguel," she said, sounding breathless. "Are you all right?"

"Yes, Mother. And so is Jose Antonio. The doctor said that if there was no change I could take him home in the morning."

"Gracias a Dios." For a moment she couldn't speak, then she asked, "Has Emma arrived?"

"A little while ago. We'll all come home together tomorrow."

"I'm glad she is with you."

"Yes," he said. "So am I."

He went back to the room after he changed his clothes. Emma was sitting in a chair by the bed, and now it was she who was holding Jose's hand. She looked up and saw him. And smiled. "He's better," she whispered. "I'm sure he's much better."

All through that long night the two of them sat beside the little boy. Sometimes they talked, sometimes they were silent. But even in the silence there was comfort.

When Jose woke, Miguel held him while Emma spooned hot soup into his mouth. She spoke softly to the boy, telling him how brave he was, encouraging him to have another spoonful of soup, a sip of hot chocolate. She was quiet and calm and loving. And though Miguel had known how fine she was, he had never really thought of her in quite this way.

In his mind Emma was the typical North American woman, capable and self-sufficient, comfortable in her own environment, city bred and wearing smart city clothes. Yet here she was in this small out-of-the-way hospital, wearing his mother's severe black clothes, holding his little son's hand.

This was a side of Emma he had never seen before, and he knew that yet another facet had been added to their relationship. Before, there had been passion and a growing affection. Now he was seeing her strength and her compassion. It meant more to him than he could ever tell her.

The hour grew late. The radio was turned off; the corridors were silent. When Jose Antonio murmured in his sleep, it was Emma who said, "Everything is all right, *niño*. Your *papá* is here and so am I. Sleep, darling. Sleep now."

Miguel took her hand and together, all through that long night, they kept their vigil beside the little boy's bed.

Jose Antonio was hungry when he awoke the next morning. When his breakfast was brought to him he wrinkled his nose at the *atole,* that pasty liquid that all Mexicans believe is the perfect remedy for any ailment, and instead ate one of the sandwiches his grandmother had sent, along with a cup of hot chocolate.

A doctor came in to check on him and a nurse removed the IV. "He's going to be fine," the doctor said. "He can go home, but I'd like him to take it easy for a few days." He frowned at Miguel. "You look in worse shape than he does, Señor Rivas. I suggest that you take it easy also."

Miguel shrugged. "I'm fine," he said. "As long as I know my son is all right."

"He is," the doctor assured him. "You and your wife can take him home any time now."

His wife. That gave Miguel pause. He looked at Emma, then quickly away, hoping she hadn't understood the doctor's words.

But Emma had understood. She'd also seen Miguel's discomfort. And she knew that she had been right—there was no room in his life or in his heart for another woman.

Emma's parents left at the end of the week.

"Being here has been quite an experience," her father said. "I'm glad I got to know Miguel and his children." He grinned. "His mother, too. She's one tough old bird."

"It takes one to know one," Emma answered with a smile.

James laughed. "I've got a feeling her bark is worse than her bite."

"Maybe, but I'm not going to offer my hand to find out."

"She loves her grandchildren," Penelope said. "I know she doesn't show it, but she does. I went into Angelina's room to check on her the night we stayed there. It must have been after two, and Maria Leticia was sitting in a rocking chair beside Angelina's bed."

She took her daughter's hand. "It's difficult for some people to show or to say how much they care, Emma. Those of us to whom the words come easily need to understand that and to love even when they aren't said."

But if the love wasn't there? Sudden tears stung Emma's eyes.

"What is it, dear?" Penelope asked.

"I don't think he can love me, Mama. I think the memory of his wife and the love of his children are all Miguel needs."

"But he cares about you," Penelope said.

"Not enough. Not the way I want him to." Emma began to pace the length of her small living room. "I'll be through here in another week or two. I'll leave when I am."

Penelope shook her head. "I don't think Miguel will let you go."

"Yes, he will." Emma looked at her mother through her tears. "Yes, he will," she said.

She and Miguel took her mother and father to the airport.

"I'd like to come back when all of the artifacts are taken out of the tomb," James told Miguel. "I still think they belong in a museum, you know."

"So do I," Miguel answered. "In a *Mexican* museum." He held his hand out, and when James took it, he said, "There's no way I can thank you enough for helping Jose and me. I'm not sure we would have made it without you."

"You would have." James gripped his hand. "Look after Emma," he said. "She's very precious to her mother and to me."

And to me, Miguel almost said. But didn't.

Emma kissed her parents goodbye, and when they stepped into the jetway, Miguel put his arm around her. "They're nice people," he said. "I'm glad I had a chance to get to know them." He smiled down at her. "You're going to miss them."

"I'm going home in two weeks. I'll see them then."

"You're going home?"

"I should finish the articles this week. Then I want to take a few more photographs at Monte Alban and

I'll be finished. Anyway, Señor Sauto, the man I rented the apartment from, will be back in Oaxaca by then.''

"But I thought..." Miguel hesitated. He wasn't sure what he thought, he only knew that he didn't like the idea of Emma's leaving, at least not this soon. She'd talked about it before, but he hadn't really listened. Now here she was telling him that in two weeks she would be gone.

He wanted to argue with her, wanted to grab her and shake her and say, "I don't want you to leave." Instead he said, "We'll talk about it over dinner."

They went to one of the restaurants that overlooked the *zocalo,* where they grilled red snapper with fresh asparagus and white wine. A guitarist sang sentimental love songs. And they did not talk about Emma's leaving after all.

Nor did they talk about it when they returned to her apartment.

Miguel kissed her the moment they closed the door. "It's been too long," he said against her lips. "I've missed you, Emma. I want you."

Emma tightened her arms around him. The feel of his body close to hers warmed and excited her. "And I've missed you," she whispered. Taking his hand, she led him into the bedroom.

Hands fumbling in their haste, they undressed each other. He unzipped the back of her dress, and swore under his breath when the zipper stuck. Finally he pulled it down and she stepped out of it.

She unbuttoned his shirt while he undid her bra. Then he pulled her into his arms so that he could feel her bare breasts against his chest. He kissed her and his body grew hard with need.

Emma slipped her panties down, then reached to tug at Miguel's belt, to unzip his pants. And while they still kissed, she slid her thumbs under the elastic of his black briefs and tugged them down over his hips.

They stood close together, their bodies touching.

He cupped her bottom, opening his legs to bring her even closer. She was warm against him, and soft, so soft.

"Emma." Her name was a whispered plea against her lips. He moved his body against hers and when she began to whisper her need, he sighed with the knowledge that she wanted this as much as he did.

He caressed her breasts and ran a thumb across the peaked tips. He touched his tongue to hers and thrilled when she answered his touch. His hand ran down her body and when he felt her hot and moist and knew he could not wait, he picked her up and carried her to the bed. Their bed.

He kissed her mouth, her breasts. And all the while she touched him, touched him until it was past bearing and he raised himself over her. He looked into her eyes. "Sweet love," he whispered, and with a hoarse cry gripped her hips and joined his body to hers.

She lifted her body to his, moving with him, riding with him. When he quickened his pace, she quickened hers. When he slowed, she slowed, though it was an agony to do so.

He hungered for her mouth and took it. She rubbed her breasts against his chest. She nipped the skin of his shoulder and healed it with her mouth.

The pace quickened. He said her name in a growing agony of pleasure, and she answered, "Oh, yes, my darling. Yes."

Darling. The word touched his very soul, and he wanted to make her his forever and never let her go.

She said, "Oh, please," and her body began to tremble as she moved toward that final threshold of passion. And with the knowledge that she was this way because of him he was filled with excitement, a gladness of heart. He reveled in her passion, in the lips that quivered under his and the body that moved so hotly and sweetly against him. When the final moment came he cried her name and held her, his body shaking with reaction.

He kissed her tremulous lips. *"Querida,"* he whispered. *"Mi querido amor."*

But still he did not say the words she longed so much to hear.

Chapter 14

It had been a night of love. Hungry after so many nights without Emma, Miguel had claimed her again and again. Each time he awakened her with kisses she had come willingly into his arms. Still drowsy with sleep, she'd pressed her body to his and welcomed him with whispered words of love. Early this morning, while she still slept, he had come to a decision.

He looked at her now, sitting across the breakfast table from him, looking sleepy and well loved. "We need to talk," he said. "About your leaving."

"Yes," she answered. "I guess we should."

"I don't want you to. To leave, I mean." He cleared his throat. "I want you to stay in Oaxaca with me. I want us to live together."

"Live together?"

He reached across the table for her hand. "So that we can get to know each other better. To spend more time with each other."

"How . . . how much time?"

"Well, I—I don't know." He shook his head as though not understanding. "I care a great deal for you, Emma."

She put her cup down on the saucer. "Yes," she said. "I know. But I'm not sure. . ." She looked down at the hand that held hers. "I'm not sure that's good enough, Miguel."

His expression changed. His whole body grew still. "I don't know what you mean," he said carefully.

"Living together. That—that isn't what I want." She clenched her hands, then nibbled at her lip before she forced herself to go on. But it was hard. She loved him so much, and because she did, she wanted a commitment, not for just a few months but for a lifetime. But he wasn't ready, might never be ready.

"I don't think you're ready to make a commitment," she said, and reached for his hand again. "Believe me, I understand. I know that some people can love only once in their lives, and if that love is lost there can never be another to replace it."

His eyebrows drew together. "What are you talking about?"

"You and Yolanda."

"Yolanda?"

"I know now how much you must have loved her, how terrible it must have been when you lost her. I respect that love, Miguel, but I don't think I can compete with it."

He shoved his chair back, scraping the scarred linoleum and making a harsh sound. As harsh as his voice when he said, "I never loved Yolanda."

"But you... But I thought..." Emma stared at him, unbelieving, her eyes wide with shock. "She was your first love," she managed to say. "I thought you still loved her, her memory. I thought that was why—"

"No!" His dark eyes were intense with all that he was feeling—anger, and frustration, and yes, guilt, even after all these years, because he hadn't loved his wife. They had been married, she had given him his children, but he had never loved her. Now here was Emma, the woman who meant more to him than any woman ever had, telling him she wouldn't live with him because of what he might still feel for Yolanda.

"You don't understand the way it was," he said in a quietly restrained voice. "I was seventeen. I'd never been with a woman." He began to pace. "There was a festival in Dos Santos, some saint's day, with a carnival during the day and music and dancing and fireworks that night. We boys were horsing around, flirting with girls, chasing them. Everybody was laughing, having a good time." He looked at Emma, then away. "I chased Yolanda out behind the church, where the trees were. She was giggling...it was fun, just fun. She tripped and fell and I fell on top of her. We kissed, and then we were rolling around on the grass and all of a sudden we were breathing hard and..." He lifted his shoulders in a helpless gesture. "And it happened.

"I remember..." He closed his eyes, reliving that moment that had changed his life. "I remember hear-

ing the music from the festival and seeing the sky light
up with a burst of fireworks.''

Emma closed her eyes and tried to see him as he'd
been then. Tall for his age, probably. All arms and legs
and raging hormones, eager for sex, for everything life
had to offer.

''You can't imagine what it's like to be a seventeen-
year-old boy who has finally experienced sex,'' he went
on. ''I felt like I had just discovered something nobody else in the world knew about. I couldn't believe
what I'd been missing or that there were dozens, hundreds, thousands of women somewhere out in the
world just waiting for a macho guy like me. In the
meantime there was Yolanda.''

He shook his head. ''Poor Yolanda was terrified.
She cried because she knew she was going to hell and
because if her father ever found out what she'd done
he'd kill her.''

He stopped pacing, and looking at Emma, said,
''She thought she was pregnant. We were both scared
out of our wits. We didn't know what to do. Finally
she told her parents and they told my parents. My
mother called her a *puta*.'' He looked at Emma, his
expression bitter with all that he was feeling. ''We got
married,'' he said, ''and a week later Yolanda discovered she wasn't pregnant after all. But it was too late.
We were trapped in a marriage neither of us wanted.''

Emma wished she could say something to comfort
his obvious distress, but she didn't know what. And so
she waited.

He ran a hand through his hair. ''We moved in with
my mother, and that was difficult for Yolanda. She
was only seventeen, living in the home of a woman

who didn't like her. She was afraid of sex, afraid of me, but...suffering me because a priest had said it was her duty. I finished school in Oaxaca and I managed to get a *beca*, a scholarship to the university in Mexico City. I wanted Yolanda to go with me, but she refused and moved in with her parents for the two years I was away."

He sat down at the table and clasped his hands in front of him. "We'd been using birth control before, but when I came back to Oaxaca she told me she had confessed to the village priest and that he'd told her it was a mortal sin and that she must never use birth control again. She got pregnant with Jose Antonio and two years later with Angelina."

For a long time he didn't speak. Then he said, "I was a faithful husband, Emma. And I was sorry when Yolanda died. She was a good woman, a simple, honest woman who did the best she could. I respected her and I respected our vows. But I didn't love her."

"Then why...?" She shook her head, not understanding.

He took her two hands between his own. "I'm hesitant about marriage," he said quietly. "Not because of my undying love for Yolanda but because I'm afraid of being trapped again."

For a few moments Emma didn't say anything. She looked down at the hands that held hers. They were strong hands, tender hands. She ran her thumb across the back of one of them. She loved this man. With all her heart she loved him.

"Come live with me," he said. "Maybe in time..." His eyes were tortured. "I care about you, Emma. I don't want to lose you."

Tears flooded her eyes as she pulled her hands away from his. "I can't," she said. "I'm sorry."

As sorry as death, for surely this was as painful as dying. For she was losing a part of herself, the part she had given to him.

"Emma—"

"No." She stopped him. Then, because it needed to be said, she went on, "I love you, Miguel. I think you love me, but if you don't, or if whatever it is you feel for me isn't strong enough to bind us together, then we have nothing."

The tears that had flooded her eyes spilled down her cheeks. "I want to be like your grandmother," she managed to say. "I want to be married to you. I want to lie beside you for the next sixty years, to go to sleep with you and awaken with you. I want..." She pressed a hand to her mouth, unable to go on.

She pushed her chair back and stood. "I need to be alone for a little while," she said.

"Emma..." He reached for her, then a sigh shuddered through him and his arms dropped to his sides. "We'll talk about this again," he said.

She shook her head and went over to the window, where she stood with her back to him, arms across her chest as though she was holding herself together.

"Can I see you tonight?" he asked, his voice quietly controlled.

"I don't think so."

He took a step toward her, then stopped. "I can't help the way I feel," he said.

"Nor can I."

He moved toward the door. He stopped there and looked back at her. He started to speak. But after all, what was there to say? Without a word he went out and closed the door behind him.

Emma stood where she was, listening to his footsteps retreating down the hall. A sob escaped her throat. She turned so that he wouldn't see her at the window, and like a person suddenly blind, staggered across the kitchen to the bedroom and threw herself on the bed.

Silent tears fell. Because she had lost him. Because she couldn't change the way she was. And neither could he.

She wept because she would leave him. And because he would let her go.

Five days passed. Emma finished the series of articles she had been working on.

She made a plane reservation to fly back to Denver.

She did not hear from Miguel.

On the day before she was to leave she decided to go back one more time to Monte Alban. She needed to take some more photographs. She needed to say goodbye to Miguel.

Señor Sauto, the photographer she had rented the apartment from, stopped in to see her just as she was leaving. She told him she would vacate the apartment the following day.

He looked around. "You've done a lot with it," he said. "It looks better now than it did when you moved in."

He asked her to dinner. She refused.

It was almost two before he left. When he did she changed from the dress she'd been wearing into jeans

and a white silk shirt. She looked down at the necklace Miguel had bought for her in the museum at
Monte Alban. She touched it with loving fingers, then
slipped it over her head. It was an expensive gift, and
though she loved it, she felt it was only right to return
it to Miguel.

With a sigh she slung two of her cameras over her
shoulder and picked up her camera bag. At the corner of her street she signaled to a passing taxi and told
him she wanted to go to Monte Alban.

"I'll only be there for an hour. I'd appreciate it if
you could come back for me."

"*Muy bien,*" he said with a nod. "*Señorita . . . ?*"

"Pilgrim," Emma said.

"I will be here," he assured her when he let her off.
"One hour, *¿sí?*"

"*Sí,*" Emma said.

She purchased her ticket and, bracing herself, went
into the museum to ask if Miguel was there. The young
woman at the information booth told her that he was
in the workshop. "Just knock on the door," she said.
"Someone will let you in."

Quickly, before she could change her mind, Emma
crossed to the back of the museum, and when she saw
the tall wooden doors, she knocked.

A young man opened the doors. "*¿Sí?*" he asked.
"Can I help you, *señorita?*"

Emma cleared her throat. "I'd like to see Señor Rivas," she said.

"Señor Rivas? Of course. *Un momento.* Wait here,
please."

She heard voices, footsteps. He came, wiping his hands on a dark cloth. "Emma?" He sounded surprised. "Come in."

"No, I..." She shook her head. "I thought you'd be working in the tomb."

"There's been some trouble. A section of the roof started to crumble. It's dangerous and has to be shored up before we can proceed."

"Well, I..." She hesitated. "I'm leaving tomorrow, Miguel. I just wanted to say goodbye."

"Tomorrow?" It rocked him. "But you can't! It's too soon. I mean... I thought you'd be here through the end of the month."

"Señor Sauto's back in Oaxaca. He needs the apartment." She lifted her shoulders. "I just came out today to have one last look around." She indicated the cameras. "To take a few more photographs and to..." This was harder than she had thought it would be. She fought for control and held out her hand. "To say goodbye."

"Emma..." He felt as though he was drowning, as though the final curtain on his life was closing. "We can't leave it like this," he said. "I can't let you..." He sucked in air. "We'll have dinner tonight. We'll talk about it then."

Emma shook her head. "I don't think so, Miguel."

"Please," he said. "I can finish up here in an hour or so. I'll wait for you. Come back when you've finished."

"I'm having a taxi come for me in an hour."

"I'll take care of it."

One more night, she thought. Dinner. That's all. She wouldn't change her mind about leaving. "All right," she said at last. "I'll meet you here in an hour."

He still had hold of her fingers. She slipped them out of his and put her hand in her pocket. "I'll be back," she said.

She wished when she left him that she hadn't told him she'd meet him. Being with him again would only make things harder for both of them.

Head down, troubled by all that she was feeling, Emma walked toward the ruins. The pyramid, that ghostly monument from the past, rose high above her. She looked up at it for a long time, for the last time, engraving it into her memory, seeing once again in her mind's eye the way Miguel had looked emerging from the clouds.

Her cloud man.

She turned away from the pyramid. For a little while, mesmerized by the beginning of love, she had visualized this ancient place as wondrously exciting and mysterious. Now she saw it only as a dead city. A place of lost dreams, of ghosts that drifted away like the clouds that once again covered the top of the pyramid.

Filled with sadness and a sense of despair unlike any she had ever known, Emma began taking pictures. She photographed the ball court, the south and north platforms. She went to the tomb where she had first seen the God of Renewal, and when she went inside she stood before him as she had done the first time she had been there. She touched the stern stone face and a shiver ran through her.

"Goodbye," she said in a voice that trembled with all she was feeling. At the entrance she turned back for one last look, then, with a sense of loss she could not explain, went back into the sunlight.

Thunderclouds had gathered while she had been in the tomb, forecasting another summer storm. In a few minutes she was going to meet Miguel, but first she wanted another look at the newly discovered tomb. He had said they needed to shore up the roof. She wouldn't go in, but she would take a photograph from the outside.

There was a sudden roll of thunder, and what tourists there were headed for the exit. Emma waited until they were out of sight before she went toward the section of trees that hid the tomb from view. When she got closer she took one of her cameras and, looking through the viewfinder, focused and snapped . . . just as two men came out of the tomb. They glanced at her, then at each other.

"*¿Qué pasa?*" one of them said. "What do you think you're doing?"

"I'm sorry," Emma replied in Spanish. "I didn't know anyone was here. I just wanted to. . ." She saw the satchel that one of them was carrying, the wicker basket in the other man's arms. And she knew, suddenly she knew that they were stealing the artifacts.

She backed away. Though her lips felt frozen and her mouth was dry, she made herself smile and say, "Sorry. I know this is off-limits. I just wanted. . ." She backed up another step.

"*¡Espere!* Wait!" The man with the satchel started toward her. To the other man he said, "*¡Agárrala!* Grab her! Get the camera!"

She turned and ran through the trees in the direction of the grassy plain.

"Help!" she screamed. Where was the guard? He should have been here. Where...? She screamed again, but there was no one to hear.

A tree limb brushed her. She dodged around it and sprinted ahead. They were right behind her. One of them grabbed her shoulder. She spun away. He grabbed the strap of the camera case, jerking her back. The strap broke and the case fell.

The man who'd held the satchel spun her around. She struck out at him, hitting him hard with her fist.

He swore and reached for her. She cried out again and he clapped a hand over her mouth. She struggled, kicking back at him, but he got an arm around her waist and held her.

"*¡Caray!*" he exclaimed to the other man. "*Qué mala suerte.* What bad luck. What are we going to do with her?"

"Give me your kerchief," the man who held her said. When he did the other man tied the scarf across her mouth. Then, grasping her wrists, he pulled her after him back toward the tomb.

"We'll put her in there. We've taken care of the day guard and paid off the night guards. No one will discover her until morning."

But the roof is crumbling, Emma's mind screamed. She struggled against her captors, trying to tell them. But the words were muffled, ineffectual.

They dragged her toward the tomb. Inside, one of them took off his belt. He grabbed her hands and tied them. He pushed her ahead of him into the murky anteroom and shoved her down in a dark corner. The other man yanked his tie off and tied her ankles together.

From somewhere near the entrance there was a clatter of rocks. "What in the hell is that?" He scrambled to his feet.

"*Quién sabe,*" the other one said. "But we'd better get out of here."

Emma struggled frantically against her bonds, against the kerchief that muffled her voice. She had to tell them about the crumbling ceiling. They couldn't leave her here! There might be a cave-in!

There was another rumble of rocks. They picked up the satchel and the basket and headed toward the entrance, ignoring her strangled cries.

She heard their retreating footsteps, a skittering of rock and stone. Then she was alone, there in the darkness of the tomb.

It was almost five when Miguel went out to wait for Emma on the steps of the museum. For the last few days he had been unable to think about anything except that she was going to leave him. Last night on his way back to the city from Monte Alban he had, without conscious thought, driven to her apartment.

He'd cursed under his breath when he realized where he was. Damn it, he told himself, he hadn't wanted to fall in love with her. But he had. The only problem was he didn't know what to do about it. Could he let her leave? Could he let her walk away from him?

Why did she have to complicate matters? Why hadn't she been willing to live with him, to give both of them a chance to be sure of how they felt?

She had told him that she loved him. That must have been difficult for her, but she'd had the courage to say the words. She was a straightforward woman, a realist, and an idealist who believed in love, marriage and children. In that order. He wasn't sure that he did.

He looked at his watch. It was five-forty. Where was she? Had she decided to leave without seeing him? He couldn't believe that. It wasn't something she would do, no matter how she felt about him. Still... He shook his head. Maybe she'd started taking pictures and forgotten the time.

He looked toward the mountains and saw the clouds rolling in, heavy and dark with the promise of rain. When he heard the roll of thunder, he left the museum and hurried down the path that led to the ruins. The storm would break in another few minutes. Where in the hell was Emma?

Miguel hastened his steps. Just as he came up over the rise of land he saw young Felipe running toward him. Trying to outrun the storm, he thought. Then Felipe waved and called out to him. "*Señor!* Señor Rivas!"

Alarmed, Miguel started to run. "What is it?" he asked when he came abreast of the young man. "What's the matter?"

"The guard. Salvador. He's been shot."

"Shot? Salvador? What are you talking about? Where?"

"This way, *señor.* Near the ball court."

Together they raced toward the ball court just as the first drops of rain began to fall.

"There he is!" Felipe cried. "There at the foot of the steps."

Salvador Rodriguez lay sprawled on the ground, his back against the stone steps.

"*Jefe,*" he managed to say when he saw Miguel. "They shot me. I . . ." He grimaced in pain.

"Take it easy." Miguel knelt beside the other man, and to Felipe he said, "Run back to the museum. Phone for an ambulance." He took his shirt off, and folding it, pressed it to the wound in Salvador's side. "Can you tell me what happened?"

"Two of them. Thought they were tourists. One wearing a suit, brown. The other one, he was tall and skinny like a stick. I went to the coffee shop. My wife was sick this morning and I didn't have a lunch. Sorry . . . sorry I left the tomb."

"It's all right, Salvador." Miguel looked over his shoulder. Where was the ambulance? The man was bleeding; he needed medical attention.

"I ordered them to stop . . . pulled my gun . . ." He looked down at the blood seeping through Miguel's shirt. "The *cabrónes* shot me."

"An ambulance is on the way. We'll get you to a hospital." Miguel gripped the wounded man's shoulder. "Did you see Señorita Pilgrim?"

Salvador looked at him, not understanding.

"The American woman," Miguel said. "Did you see her?"

"No, *jefe*. I didn't see . . . didn't see . . ." His eyes closed. His body sagged.

Miguel eased him down to the ground. Spatters of rain dampened the unconscious man's face. Miguel stood and saw Felipe and three men with a stretcher running toward him. "Hurry!" he shouted. "Over here."

They reached him. One of them knelt beside Salvador Rodriguez. He checked his wound while another man jabbed an IV needle into his arm. When that was done they lifted him onto the stretcher.

"You go along to the hospital with them, Felipe," Miguel said. "Call the police. Tell them to check the bus and train stations, the airport. One of them is wearing a brown suit. The other one is tall and thin. The police will have to check baggage for stolen artifacts."

"What about you, boss?" Felipe looked worried. "You'd better get out of the rain."

"I've got to find her," Miguel said.

"What . . . ?"

But Miguel had already turned and started running in the direction of the tomb. If Emma hadn't gone back to the city, she was still here, somewhere in the ruins. She would have known the storm was coming; maybe she headed back to the museum . . . if she had been able to.

"Dear God," he whispered. He thought of the bloody wound in Salvador's side. "Don't let anything happen to her," he prayed. "Let her be . . ." He stopped, sucking in his breath. Her camera case lay near a pile of leaves. The strap was broken. A yellow film box lay in the wet grass beside it.

Chilled with fear, Miguel stooped to pick up the case. He saw the footprints—a man's hard-heeled shoes.

The breath caught in his throat. Holy Mother; they had Emma. Where was she? Had they taken her with them as a hostage? Why hadn't anybody seen them? Tourists... He groaned. The tourists had fled because of the coming storm.

He picked up the case. His expression was tortured. He felt as though he'd never breathe properly again.

Darkness came with the lowering clouds. He looked through the trees in the direction of the tomb, hesitated a moment, then turned and ran back toward the museum.

Chapter 15

The roll of thunder sounded closer. Over it Emma could hear the pounding beat of the rain somewhere above her head. And hail, hard bits of it slashing against the stone. The thunder came closer, rolling, booming loudly, and with one terrible, jarring bolt came the crashing of rocks near the entrance.

Emma jerked in panic. Her heart beat hard against her ribs. She gave a muffled cry.

For the last hour she had been struggling with the belt that bound her hands. Her wrists were slippery now, and bleeding. But it didn't matter; she had to try to free herself. She had to get out of here.

Be calm, she told herself again and again. Miguel would find her. When she didn't show up at the museum to meet him he would come looking for her.

Unless he thought that she had decided not to wait.

Despair gripped her. She shook it off. If Miguel didn't look for her here, then surely he would go to her apartment. If he didn't see her there he would come back. Please, God, let him come back.

She wasn't claustrophobic, at least she'd never been before. But bound and gagged, scarcely able to move, with thunder crashing all around her, she felt the beginning edges of panic. She heard the clattering of rocks, slipping, sliding, filling the tomb with dusty earth, and a sob of fear rose in her throat.

Darkness surrounded her like a heavy cloak of frightening mystery; thick, impenetrable. An hour passed. Two. The storm abated. She tried to think of something, anything. The fragment of a song, the line of a poem. Miguel. The way he looked when he awoke in the morning, the lock of hair that fell over his forehead. The aroma of his skin when they made love.

She closed her eyes and tried with all her might to quell the fear of the tomb, of those ancient ones whose bones lay buried here. Please, she thought. Somebody help me, please.

She opened her eyes and saw through the darkness a shaft of golden light, and her heart leapt because she thought it was a flashlight. She tried to scream out through the scarf that bound her mouth. The cry was weak, muffled. Then she realized that what she had seen was not the beam of a flashlight but a sliver of moonlight coming in through a crack in the roof of the tomb. A moan rose in her throat, then faded. For after all, faint as it was, it was light.

She looked around. The antechamber was small, no more than seven or eight feet wide. There were still a few artifacts that, in their haste, the thieves hadn't taken, pots and urns that were cracked and broken.

On one wall was a recessed niche, and in the niche she saw the carving of a figure. And knew it to be the God of Renewal.

The moonlight shone upon his face. His slightly slanted stone eyes seemed to look intently into hers. From somewhere above her head she heard the tumble of rocks and once again panic gripped her. What if there was a cave-in? What if the rocks came down and blocked the entrance? What if they blocked off her air? Suffocated her. Sealed her in the tomb.

She looked at the face of the god. Focus on him, her mind screamed. Think about him, of the man he was. There was another skittering of rocks, but she didn't look away. She looked only at him, the god who was a man, the man who was a god. Her panic eased, her breathing steadied.

Why are you afraid? he seemed to say. I am here with you. Nothing can harm you. Only look at me. Look into my eyes and understand.

Understand... Her pulses slowed. Her body felt fluid, relaxed. Her eyes drifted close.

"I am here."

Through the silence and the darkness of the night came those three words. *"I am here."*

He came to her. He stroked her hair.

"We will be as we were."

Had the words been spoken or only imagined? Was the voice a dream of what once had been?

"My beloved. My woman."

Yes, she longed to say. Oh, yes.

He began to stroke her body, slowly, sensually. She warmed to his touch.

"Come to me and we will be as we were before."

He undid her bonds. He stripped away her clothes. She looked at him as he stood before her and saw him, tall and strong, splendid in his nakedness. His eyes were dark, his cheekbones high and sharp. His mouth no longer sensuously cruel.

She lifted her arms and welcomed him into her embrace.

He took her mouth and his lips were cool against hers.

He cupped her breasts. *"I have never forgotten the feel of them, the soft roundness beneath my fingers, the tips that harden when I touch them."*

Cold lips began to caress and to suckle. *"As it was."* His breath was a whisper, his words murmured against her skin. *"As it was."*

She was pliant in his arms, warm, giving. She touched his dark hair, stroked his muscled shoulders. And quivered at his every touch. Take me, her heart cried. For I am yours. As I once was. As I am now.

He kissed her throat with his cold lips, licked her skin with his cold tongue. Cold hands traveled down her body. Cold fingers crept to the apex of her legs. He cupped her there, caressed her there while his cold lips suckled at her breast.

"It has been so long."

"We have the now," she said.

"A moment in time."

"Our moment."

"Yes."

His fingers were cool against her flesh, yet her body grew warm beneath his touch. She whispered her pleasure and ran her hands over the broadness of his chest.

"Will you not touch me, too?"

"Oh, yes," she said. "Oh yes."

His male member throbbed hard beneath her fingers. She stroked him as he stroked her. She heard his whispered pleasure and knew that soon this throbbing part of him would be a part of her. Her hand tightened around him; she thrust her body closer to his, loving his cool touch. Loving him.

He let her go and came up over her. He lifted the gold necklace that lay between her breasts. *"You wear it for me, the gift I gave you, carved with my image so that you will remember me."*

"I will remember."

"We had so little time together."

"But we have this time."

"Beloved woman."

He kissed her and his mouth was hungry against hers. He covered her with his body and it was heaven to be with him again like this.

"My love," she whispered. "Love me now."

He gripped her hips and with a cry that seemed to come from the very depths of his soul, thrust himself into her.

She lifted herself to him, offering herself, a sacrifice to his maleness, to this man, this warrior, this god. He filled her. He moved against her, strong and sure in his masculinity, thrusting hard and deep, whispering ancient words of passion and of love. He called her by her ancient name.

When it began to be too much for her, when she knew she was close to that final moment, he stopped and covered her mouth with his.

"Go slow, my love! We must make this last... last into eternity."

Once again he began to move, slower now, pacing himself, moving with such exquisite tenderness that she felt tears spring to her eyes. It was heaven and it was hell. Agony to wait, but a pain greater than bearing to have it end.

Slowly, slowly it built once again, built to a fever pitch that had them moaning into each other's mouths. His arms tightened around her. She lifted her body to his, and together they raced toward that final glorious moment.

"I cannot bear it," she cried. "Oh, love. My love."

"Stay with me. Ride with me."

He sought her mouth and whispered ancient words. With one grand and final thrust it happened. And when it did she spun through time and space and endless years, immortal in his arms.

He held her to his breast, his body convulsed, shattered, triumphant.

"Give me your mouth. Give me your breath."

"Willingly," she whispered.

She closed her eyes. She felt him kiss her eyelids.

" Sleep, dear love."

She felt him leave. Her heart cried, "No! Don't leave me. Don't..." But sleep came stealing over her, warming her as he had warmed her.

And through the mist of a dream she heard his voice. *"Farewell, my love . . . my dearest love."*

Miguel paced up and down the confines of the police lieutenant's office. It was three in the morning. He had been there earlier to give them the details Salvador Rodriguez had passed on to him. Then he had hurried to Emma's apartment in case, after all, she had gone there. But she hadn't been there. In his heart he had known she wouldn't be.

"We've set up roadblocks and we have men at the airport, the train station and the bus stations," the officer said. "I assure you, Señor Rivas, we will catch the thieves. My men are armed and ready."

"But they've got Emma!" Miguel grasped the edge of the lieutenant's desk. "She's with them," he cried. "If your men shoot she'll be in danger."

"It is a risk we must take if we hope to catch the criminals."

"No!" Miguel pounded on the desk with his fist. "You've got to protect her. You've got to tell your men to be careful."

"They will be careful, Señor Rivas. But if we are to apprehend the criminals we must use every means at our disposal. The *Federales* are involved because the thieves have our national treasures in their possession. We cannot let them get away."

Miguel wanted to leap across the desk and grab the policeman by the throat. Instead he fought to remain calm, to speak in a reasonable voice. "Señorita Pilgrim must be your first consideration," he said. "I'm in charge of the excavation of the tomb the artifacts were taken from. They're valuable, Lieutenant, but not as valuable as a human life. If anything happens to Señorita Pilgrim . . ."

He would not allow himself to think beyond that. If indeed the two men had taken her hostage, then she was their ticket out of the area. If they got up into the mountains they would probably let her go. Probably.

Someone brought him coffee. He couldn't drink it. All he could do was pace, and hope and pray that she was all right.

There were so many things he wanted to tell her. So many things he had been afraid to say. He knew now that he loved her; he'd known all along, but he'd been afraid to say the words that would make her stay, the words that would bind her to him for a lifetime.

She had told him she wanted to be like his grandmother Rosa. "I want to live with you for sixty years," she'd said. "I want to go to sleep with you and awaken with you."

Emma, his heart cried. I want it, too. I want those sixty years. I want to live with you beside me for as long as we have.

He prayed to God, and to ancient gods. He prayed as he had never prayed before. Let her be all right. Let her be all right.

The phone rang.

"*¿Sí?*" the lieutenant shouted into it. "What? And the woman? I see. Yes, as quickly as you can." He put the phone down. "We've got them," he said. "They had the artifacts."

"And Emma?" Miguel asked in a voice that shook with all that he was feeling. "What about Emma?"

"She wasn't with them."

Miguel stared at him. "But she has to be!"

The lieutenant shook his head. "My men are bringing them in. We'll question them." His eyes narrowed. "I assure you, *señor,* they will tell us what they have done with her."

Miguel paced. He tried to drink the cold coffee. He accepted the cigarette the lieutenant offered, took two drags and crushed it out. When he heard a commotion in the corridor he ran toward it.

Two officers, backed by three others, brought the two men in.

Miguel grabbed the one in the brown suit before any of the officers could stop him. "Where is she?" he shouted. "What have you done with her?"

The man tried to break free of Miguel's grip. But Miguel yanked him back. "Where's the woman?" he roared.

"Go to hell!"

Miguel hit him. Brown Suit staggered back, slammed into the wall, slid down and landed hard. Before he could recover, Miguel was on him.

"¡Bastardo!" he cried. "Tell me where she is!"

"Get him off me!" The man held his hands up to cover his face.

Miguel hit him again. "Where is the woman?" he roared.

"In the tomb."

Miguel hauled him to his feet. "The tomb?" Oh, my God, he thought. The tomb! In a low and deadly voice he said, "If you have hurt her I'll kill you."

"We didn't hurt her," the other man said. "I swear we didn't touch her."

"*¡Cabrón!*" Miguel shoved Brown Suit toward one of the officers before he turned and sprinted toward the door. The lieutenant and one of his men ran after him.

"Get in the squad car," the lieutenant said. "We'll make better time with the siren going."

Miguel hesitated for only an instant before he jumped into the front seat. "Hurry," he cried. "*Por Dios,* hurry!"

The moon had disappeared when Emma opened her eyes. There was no shaft of silver light, only darkness. Her arms and legs were bound, the kerchief covered her mouth. She was alone.

In that state between sleep and wakefulness her heart cried out to him, "Where are you? Where have you gone? Oh, please, come back. Come back to me!"

Had it only been a dream? Or was the here and now the dream, and what had happened, the reality?

She began to weep, not with the fear she had known before, but because he had left her. Because she knew somehow that he would never return.

In the darkness of the lonely night she tried to call him back to her. With her bound hands she touched the necklace he had touched and found it warm from the heat of her breasts.

A crack of thunder split the silence. With the sound came the crashing of great stones, stones that would cover the opening of the tomb. They would cut off her air. By the time Miguel and his workers found her she would be dead, sealed for all eternity here with him.

She closed her eyes, and a sense of peace unlike any she had ever known calmed and quieted her.

I will be with him, she thought. With him.

The sharp wail of the siren cut through the night air. A streak of lightning split the lowering clouds and thunder rolled. The earlier storm had passed; another was on its way.

"Faster!" Miguel said. "Can't you go any faster?"

The driver pressed down on the accelerator and the speedometer needle jumped to seventy-five miles per hour.

Horn blowing, siren blaring, they shot through the city, running red lights, darting around the few cars that were still on the road at this hour. Behind them came another police car and an ambulance.

They reached the turnoff and started the climb up toward Monte Alban. The driver slowed to thirty-five around the first curve, got up to fifty on the short straightaway, then cut to thirty to take another curve.

Miguel's hands were knotted into fists. He thought about the section of the tomb's roof that needed shoring up. It was dangerous, so dangerous that neither he nor his helpers had gone inside for the last two days. They were going to start shoring up tomorrow. God! Tomorrow!

He felt as though his insides were filled with ground glass, as though he couldn't get his breath. There was the sickness of fear in him. Fear for Emma. Dear God, Emma.

The road was dark, dangerous, winding. All he could see was the reflection of the red light whirling on the top of the police car. Other than that there was only darkness.

Like the darkness of the tomb. He thought of her there alone in the dark, sealed off from light, tied and trapped. He felt her fear and knew it was his own. If there was a cave-in . . . No! Please God, no. He would get to her in time. Take her out of the tomb. Never let her go.

"We're almost there," the lieutenant said from the back seat.

They pulled into the parking lot. Miguel was out of the car before it stopped.

"Wait," the lieutenant called, and shoved a flashlight into his hands.

Miguel raced up the steps leading to the museum and started toward the rise of hill that led to the site, not waiting for the men who ran behind him. In a sudden crack of lightning that illuminated the sky, he saw the pyramid rising up before him. He thought of Emma, of the night they had made love there. That first glorious time.

Tonight there was no whisper of wind, no nighthawks flying high against the moon.

He ran for the trees that hid the tomb. He swore and called himself every kind of a fool because he had been here earlier and had not looked inside. She had been there, bound and helpless, and he had not gone in.

He reached the entrance. Rocks were piled high against the opening. He shoved the flashlight into his pocket and began to claw at them.

"Emma!" he shouted. "Emma!"

But there was no answering cry.

What if the roof had caved in? What if she were trapped and bleeding, maybe dead under a pile of rocks? With renewed frenzy he heaved the rocks aside.

The others reached him. They shone their flashlights over the entrance and without a word they, too, began to grab at the rocks. When they'd cleared a place big enough for a man to crawl through, Miguel said, "I'm going in. Keep clearing."

He squeezed through the narrow opening, then he was inside and able to stand. He shone his flashlight around. Emma wasn't there. He called her name again, and heard a muffled cry.

He ran into the antechamber, flashed his light around the walls and saw her, in a corner, her back against the wall.

Then he was beside her, cradling her in his arms, holding her as though he'd never let her go.

She tried to speak, but only muffled sounds came out. He realized then that her mouth was bound. He said, "Sorry, *querida*. Sorry." And untied the kerchief.

She said his name, then she was in his arms again. He touched her face, her arms. "You're not hurt?" he cried. "They didn't hurt you?"

"No, Miguel, but please, please get me out of here."

There was the sound of rocks being cleared and of other voices.

"In here," Miguel called. He lifted Emma to her feet. He untied her wrists and her ankles, then picked her up and carried her to the entrance.

The opening had been cleared. He lifted her through it. She clung to him, and took great gulps of the fresh night air.

"We'd better get her to a hospital," someone said.

Emma shook her head. "No, please. I don't want to go to a hospital."

"All right," he said. "I'll take you home with me, my love."

And with his arm still around her, and the others following behind, he led her toward the parking lot.

It wasn't until they were in his condo that he saw her bloody wrists. While he ran a tub of hot water, he bathed and bound the cuts, wincing when Emma winced, feeling the pain as she felt it.

When the tub was filled he undressed her. He helped her into the water, then knelt on the floor beside her.

"I thought they had taken you as a hostage," he told her. "When the police found the thieves and brought them in, when you weren't with them, I thought..." He stopped. He would not tell her that he had pictured her in some mountain gulley or arroyo, frightened, hurt. Or worse.

"They told us they'd left you in the tomb," he said.

"I was taking pictures," Emma told him. "I saw them just as they came out of the tomb. One was carrying a satchel, the other had a basket. I knew they'd taken the artifacts. I tried to get away but they caught me. They tied my ankles and my wrists...." She shuddered and closed her eyes.

"It's all right," Miguel said. "You're safe now, Emma. You're with me."

He began to bathe her. He washed her back and her arms, careful not to touch the injured wrists. When that was done he washed her face, then gently wiped away the soap. He lathered his hands and then her breasts.

She leaned back against the tub. With her eyes closed she let him minister to her.

When he helped her out of the tub he dried her body with a soft white towel.

"I can do it," she protested.

But Miguel shook his head. "Let me take care of you," he said. "I need to."

He wrapped her in a terry cloth robe and led her into his bedroom. He removed the heavy raw silk spread and turned back the sheets. He helped her in and lay down beside her.

It was almost morning. He drew her into his arms.

"I've never been afraid of the dark before," Emma whispered. "But it was so dark in the tomb, Miguel." She shivered in his arms. "The rocks kept tumbling. I could hear them and I was afraid the entrance would be blocked, afraid the roof would fall."

He brought her closer. "It must have been terrible for you alone there in the darkness."

"But I wasn't alone. He..." She stopped and drew in her breath.

Miguel looked down at her. "What?" He looked puzzled. "What do you mean, *querida?*"

"I. ." She shook her head, and knew that she would never tell him. "It was a dream," she said. "I had a dream." She touched his face. "And when I woke up I heard your voice and knew that I was safe."

She rested her head against his shoulder. "Don't leave me," she said. "I don't want to be alone in the dark."

"You'll never be alone," he whispered. And held her while she slept.

Chapter 16

Two days later workers began shoring up the walls of the tomb. It was a miracle, they said, that they hadn't collapsed.

"Especially in the antechamber," one of the engineers told Miguel. "Centuries of rain has crumbled the mortar. One of the walls was ready to go, and if it had, the others would have gone, too. I'll never know what prevented it."

Nor did Miguel. He knew how precariously close he had come to losing Emma. And because he knew, he couldn't bear to let her out of his sight. As soon as she had rested and regained her strength he said, "I'm taking you to the *choza* for a few days."

"But I have an airline reservation," she protested.

"Cancel it. You've had a bad experience. You need time to recover."

He refused to listen to all the reasons why she had to go back to Denver. Though she argued, he remained adamant. They were going to the *choza*.

He helped her package her articles and photographs, and mailed them to her publisher. He stood by while she phoned her parents to tell them she was staying in Mexico for another few weeks. He shopped for the supplies they would need—canned food, bread and cheese, fresh fruit and vegetables.

"I'll do the cooking," he said. "All you have to do is rest."

She wanted to joke, to say, "Is that all I have to do?" But she did not. She and Miguel had reached an agreement of sorts before the incident in the tomb. He had told her his reasons for not wanting to make a commitment. And those reasons, as far as she was concerned, had not changed. She would stay with him for this little while, then she would leave and that would be the end of it.

But for now, she decided, for this little time they would be together. And so she let herself relax and go along with his plans.

Three days after her ordeal in the tomb, they left the city and drove to the *choza*.

As he had before when they had been there, Miguel worked in the mornings. This time, because her work was finished, Emma read or pottered in the vegetable garden alongside the house. Every afternoon they took long walks. They slept together at night, but they did not make love.

The first time he took her in his arms, she said, "I'm tired, Miguel. And nervous. I'm sorry. I—I'd just like to go to sleep."

But she did not sleep well. She had terrible nightmares about being alone in the tomb, and often she awoke trembling and crying out with fear. When that happened, Miguel was there to hold her and tell her that she was safe.

"You're here with me, *querida,*" he soothed. "Nothing will hurt you now."

And once, between sleeping and waking, she cried, "Come back! Oh, please, come back!"

"I'm here," Miguel said. "Emma, I'm here."

She opened her eyes and a look of unutterable sadness crossed her face, and her body shivered as though with a chill.

"I'm sorry," she whispered. "Sorry."

Sometimes when she was alone she would think of that night in the tomb. She would touch the gold necklace that he had touched and remember the coolness of hands on her body, the lips that had kissed her lips.

Once Miguel came upon her in the garden, sitting on the old stone bench his grandfather had built for his grandmother so long ago. Her lips were curved in a bittersweet smile, her hands were open, palms up, upon her lap.

"Emma?" he said.

She turned to look at him. And it seemed to him that for the barest fraction of an instant she didn't recognize him. Then she shook her head as though to clear it and said, "I must have been dreaming."

He took her empty hands, and as he held them he felt an unreasoning fear, because in a way he could not explain it seemed to him that Emma was somehow drifting away from him. Something was different. He didn't know what it was, but it scared the hell out of him.

He wanted to tell her all he had been feeling since that terrible night when he'd been afraid she was lost from him forever, but he was put off by the feeling that she was so preoccupied with her thoughts that she wouldn't hear him.

Then one night she said, "We've been here for a week. It's time I went home, Miguel."

He took a breath to steady himself. "I don't want you to go, Emma."

"We've already discussed this," she said with a gentle smile. "I understand how you feel."

"No, you don't." He shook his head, and knew that this was the time to tell her. "I've changed," he said. "I knew the night I found you in the tomb how much you meant to me."

He came to her. He knelt on the floor beside the sofa. "I love you, Emma," he said. "I want to marry you." He took her hands and kissed them. "You said you wanted to be like my grandmother, that you wanted to be married to me for sixty years. That's what I want too, my dear. I want to be married to you and to love you for as long as I live."

She smoothed a lock of hair back from his forehead. "Oh, darling," she said. "I don't think so."

He was as stunned as he would have been if she had struck him. "But it's what you wanted," he protested. "Now it's what I want, too. If you're angry because I backed off at the idea of marriage—"

"I'm not angry, Miguel."

He shook his head. "Then what is it?"

She slipped her hands from his. "I don't know," she said. "I can't tell you. I—I don't think I'll ever marry."

He stared at her. Then slowly got to his feet and turned his back on her.

"I'm so sorry," she said.

His shoulders stiffened. Without a word he went out and closed the door.

Emma slumped back on the sofa. She had hurt him and she hadn't meant to. What was the matter with her? Ten days ago she would have given anything she had to have Miguel ask her to marry him. But now... She shook her head. She didn't understand. How could she tell him? How could she say, because I'm in love with a ghost from the past. With a warrior god who returned to possess me for one unbelievable night. Because no one, my darling, not even you, has touched me the way he did. Because I will never forget him. Because if I have to I'll wait a lifetime for him to come back to me.

Miguel strode through the fields, kicking at clods of dirt, sending small animals scurrying in fear. He didn't know what was the matter with Emma. She had changed since that night in the tomb and he didn't know why. Certainly it had been a bad experience for her. She'd been frightened and with very good reason. But that didn't account for her not wanting to marry him. If she was trying to punish him... No,

Emma wouldn't do that. It was something else. It had to be something else.

It was late by the time Miguel returned to the cabin. Emma was in bed, the lamp on the dresser glowing.

"Are you asleep?" he asked when he went in.

"No." She sat up and leaned back against the pillows. Before, when there had been closeness between them, she had not worn nightgowns. But she wore them now. Nightgowns and the gold necklace.

Tonight she wore an old-fashioned white cotton gown with a lace trim around the neck. Her hair was loose about her shoulders. She had never looked more beautiful, more desirable.

"We have to talk," he said. "I have to know what's going on."

Her eyebrows came together in the beginning of a frown. "I don't know what you mean."

"You've changed, Emma." He sat beside her on the edge of the bed. "I know the experience in the tomb spooked you. Maybe it even gave you a bad feeling about being here—in Mexico, I mean."

She shook her head. "I don't think so."

He began again. "Before the incident in the tomb you told me that you loved me."

"I did. I mean I do."

"Do you?"

"Yes, of course."

"Then why won't you marry me?"

"I don't know. I—I need more time."

"How much time? A month? Six months? A year?"

"Miguel..." She covered his hand with hers. "I just don't know. Maybe you're right. Maybe something did happen to me that night in the tomb." She lifted her shoulders in a helpless gesture. "I need time to sort things out."

"I see." He got up. "Would you rather I spent the night on the sofa?"

"No, of course not."

He turned the lamp off and undressed in the dark, then, naked, got into bed beside her.

For a few moments neither of them spoke. "I'm so sorry," she said at last. "I don't know why I feel like I do. I'm not sure I understand any better than you do."

"You know I love you." He turned on his side to look at her. "I'm sorry I didn't tell you before. But know that it's true. I do love you."

"I know, Miguel."

They lay without touching, both with their troubled thoughts, both unhappy. In a little while she went to sleep, and, finally, so did Miguel.

He wasn't sure what awakened him—the rustle of an animal on the roof, the call of a night bird. He only knew that suddenly he was wide awake, that every part of his body was vibrating with life, and that he wanted Emma with an intensity such as he had never known.

He touched her shoulder. "Emma?" he whispered. "Emma?" But she didn't stir.

He could wait until morning. Perhaps then... No. He couldn't wait. The feeling was too intense. Too overpowering.

He drew her into his arms and kissed her. She murmured in her sleep and her lips parted under his.

He stroked her breasts. She sighed and moved closer.

"*¿Querida?*" he whispered against her lips. He took her hand and guided it to him. "This is how much I want you," he said.

Her hand tightened around him. Her fingers reached to stroke.

"That's it," he whispered. "That's it, my Emma." He feathered kisses over her breasts. And heard her whispered pleasure. He took a hardened peak between his teeth to tug and tease and kiss. He reveled in the taste of her, in the trembling of her body so close to his.

Dios, how he'd wanted her! *Dios,* how he loved her! She was his *mujer,* his woman, his light, his sun, the very reason for his being. He took her mouth again and kissed her with an intensity that left him shaking with need.

"Emma," he whispered against her lips. "Don't leave me. *Por Dios,* don't ever leave me."

He lifted himself so he could look into her sleep-filled eyes. He touched the gold necklace that lay between her breasts and rubbed his lips across it. "I love you," he said. "Now and forever, Emma."

Then he was inside her, enveloped in her warmth, and for a moment it was enough to feel her like this, warm and moist and comforting, holding him, enclosing him, making him a part of her.

She drifted as though in a sensuous dream. She held him with soft and languid arms, and lifted her body to his when he began to move against her.

When first he touched her his hands had been cool against her flesh. Then, warmed by her, his body warmed. Now, inside her, he grew and filled her with the essence of his masculinity.

She floated on a half-remembered dream of love.

He caressed her breasts. He said, "I have never forgotten the feel of them, the soft roundness beneath my fingers, the tips that harden when I touch them."

Her eyes flew open.

His cool lips began to caress and to suckle. "As it was," he whispered.

She looked into eyes that were so like those other eyes.

"Beloved," he murmured against her lips.

Then a wildness took him and he began to move so deeply, so frantically against her that for a moment she was frightened. But only for a moment. Her fear turned to excitement and she moved as he moved, desperately reaching for that final moment, that wondrous peak of ecstasy.

But he said, "No. Wait. Go slow, my love. We must make this last—"

"Into eternity," she said.

He felt as one possessed. As though he could not get close enough to her, as though he would never get enough of her. He ground his body against hers, into hers, needing to possess her, to meld himself to her, body and bones, flesh of his flesh. His woman, now and forever.

She moved as frantically as he, holding him with her arms and with her legs, lifting her body to his.

Together they began the ascent toward that final moment, and when it came she cried aloud, and wept with exultation against his shoulder.

"My love!" he cried. "My dearest love!"

They clung to each other, their bodies shaking with reaction. "Never leave me," he said.

"I never will," she answered.

And knew that it was true.

The next morning they made their wedding plans.

"I have to call my mother and father," Emma said.

"They'll come back for the wedding?"

"Oh, yes, I'm sure they will."

She reached across the table for his hand. She did not understand what had happened to her in the tomb, or last night, or how the god of the ancients had merged with the man who was Miguel. She only knew that she loved him, the god, the man. Miguel.

"We'll look for a house in the city tomorrow," he said. "I'd like to have the children with us, but if you think it's too much right at first, that it would be better if we were by ourselves—"

"No," Emma said. "I'd like them with us."

"After our honeymoon." He smiled. "We'll go somewhere to a beach. We'll swim all day and make love all night. Would that suit you?"

"Anywhere with you would suit me." She touched his face. "Anywhere, my love."

The wedding was held the following week on the grassy plain in front of the pyramid. The priest who married them stood with his back to it. They stood where they could see it.

Emma wore a traditional white ruffled Mexican wedding dress, and baby orchids in her hair. Around her neck she wore the heavy gold necklace Miguel had given her.

Angelina stood beside her, Jose Antonio next to his father. Her parents were there, and so was Maria Leticia, who for once had put aside her traditional black dress for a softer gray.

As the priest conducted the simple service, Emma looked up at the pyramid and remembered when their love had begun. Miguel followed her gaze and tightened his hand around hers, for he, too, remembered.

As they looked up, a single hawk flew overhead. It swooped low over the pyramid and for a moment seemed to hover there, suspended in the coolness of the summer air. It called out once, a wild and keening cry, then flapped its wings and flew away.

''Poor thing,'' Miguel whispered. ''He's lost his mate.''

But someday he will find her again, Emma thought.

The priest raised a hand in benediction as he said the words uniting them as man and wife.

And Emma turned to receive her lover's kiss.

* * * * *

Silhouette
SPECIAL EDITION™

It takes a very
special man to win

That SPECIAL Woman!

She's friend, wife, mother—she's you! And beside each Special Woman
stands a wonderfully *special* man. It's a celebration of our heroines—
and the men who become part of their lives.

Look for these exciting titles from Silhouette Special Edition:

April   FALLING FOR RACHEL by Nora Roberts
Heroine: Rachel Stanislaski—a woman dedicated to her career
discovers romance adds spice to life.

May   THE FOREVER NIGHT by Myrna Temte
Heroine: Ginny Bradford—a woman who thought she'd never love
again finds the man of her dreams.

June   A WINTER'S ROSE by Erica Spindler
Heroine: Bently Cunningham—a woman with a blue-blooded
background falls for one red-hot man.

July   KATE'S VOW by Sherryl Woods
Heroine: Kate Newton—a woman who viewed love as a mere fairy tale
meets her own Prince Charming.

Don't miss THAT SPECIAL WOMAN! each month—from some of your
special authors! Only from Silhouette Special Edition! And for the most
special woman of all—you, our loyal reader—we have a wonderful gift:
a beautiful journal to record all of your special moments. Look for
details in this month's THAT SPECIAL WOMAN! title, available at your
favorite retail outlet.

TSW2

MEN MADE IN AMERICA

Fifty red-blooded, white-hot, true-blue hunks from every
State in the Union!

Beginning in May, look for MEN MADE IN AMERICA!
Written by some of our most popular authors, these
stories feature fifty of the strongest, sexiest men, each
from a different state in the union!

Two titles available every other month at your favorite
retail outlet.

In July, look for:

CALL IT DESTINY by Jayne Ann Krentz (Arizona)
ANOTHER KIND OF LOVE by Mary Lynn Baxter
(Arkansas)

In September, look for:

DECEPTIONS by Annette Broadrick (California)
STORMWALKER by Dallas Schulze (Colorado)

You won't be able to resist MEN MADE IN AMERICA!

**Relive the romance...
Harlequin and Silhouette
are proud to present**

by Request

A program of collections of three complete novels by the most requested authors with the most requested themes. Be sure to look for one volume each month with three complete novels by top name authors.

In June: **NINE MONTHS** Penny Jordan
Stella Cameron
Janice Kaiser

Three women pregnant and alone. But a lot can happen in nine months!

In July: **DADDY'S HOME** Kristin James
Naomi Horton
Mary Lynn Baxter

Daddy's Home... and his presence is long overdue!

In August: **FORGOTTEN PAST** Barbara Kaye
Pamela Browning
Nancy Martin

Do you dare to create a future if you've forgotten the past?

Available at your favorite retail outlet.

REQ-G

If you've been looking for something a little bit different,
a little bit spooky, let Silhouette Books take you on
a journey to the dark side of love with

Every month, Silhouette will bring you two romantic,
spine-tingling Shadows novels, written by some of your
favorite authors, such as *New York Times* bestseller
Heather Graham Pozzessere, Anne Stuart, Helen R. Myers
and Rachel Lee—to name just a few.

In May, look for:
FLASHBACK by Terri Herrington
WAITING FOR THE WOLF MOON by Evelyn Vaughn

In June, look for:
BREAK THE NIGHT by Anne Stuart
IMMINENT THUNDER by Rachel Lee

Come into the world of Shadows and prepare
to tremble with fear—and passion....

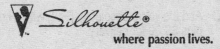

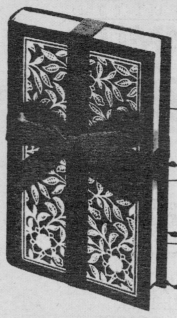